BLINDSIDE

A Selection of Titles by Ed Gorman

The Dev Conrad Series

SLEEPING DOGS
STRANGLEHOLD
BLINDSIDE *

The Sam McCain Series

THE DAY THE MUSIC DIED
WAKE UP LITTLE SUSIE
WILL YOU STILL LOVE ME TOMORROW?
SAVE THE LAST DANCE FOR ME
EVERYBODY'S SOMEBODY'S FOOL
BREAKING UP IS HARD TO DO
FOOLS RUSH IN
TICKET TO RIDE
BAD MOON RISING

* available from Severn House

BLINDSIDE

Ed Gorman

This first world edition published 2011
in Great Britain and in the USA by
SEVERN HOUSE PUBLISHERS LTD of
9–15 High Street, Sutton, Surrey, England, SM1 1DF.
Trade paperback edition first published
in Great Britain and the USA 2012 by
SEVERN HOUSE PUBLISHERS LTD.

British Library Cataloguing in Publication Data

Gorman, Edward.
  Blindside.
  1. Conrad, Dev (Fictitious character) – Fiction.
  2. Political consultants – United States – Fiction.
  3. Political campaigns – United States – Fiction.
  4. Murder – Investigation – Fiction. 5. Suspense fiction.
  I. Title
  813.5′4-dc22

ISBN-13: 978-0-7278-8025-3 (cased)
ISBN-13: 978-1-84751-395-3 (trade paper)

All Severn House titles are printed on acid-free paper.

Severn House Publishers support The Forest Stewardship Council [FSC],
the leading international forest certification organisation. All our titles that
are printed on Greenpeace-approved FSC-certified paper carry the FSC logo.

Typeset by Palimpsest Book Production Ltd.,
Falkirk, Stirlingshire, Scotland.
Printed and bound in Great Britain by
MPG Books Ltd., Bodmin, Cornwall.

PART ONE

ONE

always feel right at home when a large number of people at a political rally are carrying guns and assault weapons. I'd been planning on bringing my rocket launcher but in my hurry to get here I'd forgotten it.

And what the weapons hadn't said as yet the placards certainly made clear:

BALLOTS OR BULLETS

BLACK MAKES ME BLUE

PRESIDENT PIMP

JUST TRY & TAKE MY GUN. JUST TRY.

On a chilly but colorful fall afternoon in the small city of Atherton, Illinois, somewhere around a thousand people had gathered to hear Rusty Burkhart tell them how he was going to burn and pillage Washington, D.C. when they elected him their congressman.

He was going to start by making every sitting member of Congress sign a loyalty oath and then he was going to subpoena the private e-mails of a target list of House and Senate members he suspected of being 'anti-American.' During all this time he was going to permanently shut down the Department of Education and the Environmental Protection Agency and he was going to prove once and for all that the president was a Muslim Manchurian Candidate.

The fact that a congressman couldn't do any of these things – well, he could, I suppose, burn and pillage, but then he'd be arrested for arson and at a minimum criminal trespassing – did not keep his admirers from shouting encouragement and screaming nasty remarks about the president, who had the unmitigated gall to have been born half black. I was no longer much enamored of our president as a leader but I sure as hell felt sorry for him as a man.

Rusty Burkhart was a sixty-three-year-old multimillionaire. He was CEO and chairman of the Board of Burkhart, Inc., which owned everything from chains of supermarkets to coal mines. A man just

like you and me, as he liked to say, never mentioning that he'd gone
to Yale and owned a yacht big enough to launch an invasion.

He was also a fixture at local city council meetings. What should
have been one-hour meetings frequently stretched to three and even
four because of his rants. And he always brought at least a couple
dozen people along to help him. They loved to hiss and boo. His
main issues were taxes and money allotted for helping people at
any time and in any way. He had been quoted as saying that 'God
has a plan for poor people and it's not right to interfere with that.'

He was six-four and burly with a comic red toupee that needed
to be drowned. He was given to Western shirts and jeans with a
giant belt buckle of gold that bore a Christian cross. His most famous
piece of attire was his red, white, and blue cowboy boots. Another
Yale cowpoke who later in life began channeling John Wayne.

'This is really scary,' Lucy Cummings said to me as we stood
on the edge of the crowd sipping coffee from paper cups with George
Washington's face printed on them. 'I really hate guns.'

The coffee was surprisingly good and Lucy, whom I'd met an
hour ago, managed to forget the firearms long enough to pick up a
donut. She was in the thirty range, a slightly overweight woman in
a gray pantsuit. She had a youthful and attractive face and smoked
a lot, something far too many political operatives on both sides do.
She was one of Congressman Jeff Ward's staffers. Against my better
judgment I was working on Ward's campaign for a couple of days.
Lucy and I were checking out the competition, Mr Burkhart.

I'd tuned Burkhart's barking out and was instead trying to make
some sociological sense of all the cars parked to my right. A number
of the trucks looked as if they'd done service in the Dust Bowl
while the two Jags and large number of beemers appeared to have
been driven straight from their country clubs to here.

'This is the end of civilization, Dev, I swear to God.'

'Close. But probably not quite the end.'

'How can these people believe all this crap?'

'They will themselves to believe it. They're angry about the
economy and they gravitate to people who let them express all their
prejudices as well as vent their anger. It just about always works.'

'Hey, Conrad, where's your gun?'

And then she was there. Sylvia Fordham. 'The Boss-Bitch of
Political Consultants,' according to *Newsweek* in a piece they'd done

on her the year she brought down a congressman who'd served four terms. He'd lost both his legs in Nam but she'd found – the rumor was she'd paid them close to two hundred grand to split – four men who claimed they'd been in over there the same time he was. They not only claimed that he was a coward who'd deserted his unit, but also hinted that he was into pot and even heavier drugs the whole time he served. Add to that the fact that he was black and she was able to exploit an impoverished Southern town's racism into a landslide.

She was a small, slight woman cast in the Audrey Hepburn fashion. If she wasn't quite as luminous as Hepburn had been, she was skilled at playing the public role of the bright, quick, upper-class woman who issued her lies with quiet charm and big-eyed innocence. Off-camera her thirty-something prettiness contrasted sharply with her bitchiness. But in twelve years of battling each other's candidates I'd learned she was as ruthless as she was appealing.

'I'm surprised you'd risk your life by coming here, Dev. If I told some of these patriots who you are, they'd probably open fire.'

'Any of them able to count to ten?'

'Always the snob.' She looked at Lucy. 'I've told you before you'd be pretty if you'd dress better. After November's election, honey, you're going to be looking for a job so you'll have to spruce up your act.'

I smiled at Lucy and nodded in Sylvia's direction. 'She used to room with Mother Teresa.'

Lucy laughed nervously. 'I'll bet she did.'

'But I have to say, Dev, that I'm glad to see you here. That means the Ward people are getting desperate. Calling in a hired gun like you means they've been reading the same internal polls we have. We're running five ahead right now.'

'Three according to our internals,' Lucy said. She was still intimidated by Fordham's nastiness. Mostly I was bored with it. Her shtick had grown old long ago.

A huge response of applause and shouts rang out from around the bandstand.

'The people love him,' Sylvia said. 'They know he's one of them.'

'Yeah, I'll bet half the people in this crowd inherited ten million when they turned twenty-five. And I bet they went to Yale, too. Just a regular guy. Who, by the way, should stop wearing that shitty rug. With his money can't he find a better toupee than that?'

'I'm sure when he gets to Washington he'll find one that meets with your approval.' A guy in a suit holding a walkie-talkie waved to her.

'I've got an election to win. I hope I see you later, Dev. Dinner would be fun.' Then she gave us one of those princess waves that movie stars affect these days. 'Toodles.'

'How much time would I get for second degree?' Lucy said as Sylvia walked away.

My smile matched hers. 'They'd probably let you off with a parking fine.'

Three Iraq veterans in wheelchairs were being escorted on to the stage. Sylvia was good, paying broke soldiers to praise Burkhart. I didn't blame them. I'd have taken the money, too. The people at large and Congress had screwed these soldiers every way possible since they'd come back from that war. I just wondered if any of them had heard that Burkhart, who'd never served in the military, had said he was tired of 'pampering' veterans with government money.

There were so many large flags on stage people were getting lost in them. Burkhart led the crowd in the national anthem. I guess being off-key meant you were being sincere.

For a few minutes I allowed myself to enjoy the afternoon. I watched hawks ride the air currents and smelled the smoky scent of the breeze and saw the surrounding hills melancholy with leaves that were beautiful in their dying. This was the season of Halloween and football Saturdays and long walks to watch the shadows stretch as dusk came early now. To hell with the Burkharts and Sylvias. If they had their way they'd strip-mine and cut down everything that made the landscape godly. They'd also start revising textbooks the way Texas and a few other states already had – you know, the John Wayne mythic America. There was a time in my life when I occasionally voted for men and women of the other side. But that party and those people had no place in the opposition anymore.

I listened to Burkhart start his salutation to the whites-only world he'd grown up in. Talk about your opium for the masses as Marx said of religion. The portrait he painted of Mom and Dad, flag and country, opportunity and riches rang resonantly on the Midwestern plains. The anger at a black president and liberals and immigrants and gays would come a bit later. For now he was letting his supporters feast on this picnic lunch of treacle and bullshit.

Burkhart was a cunning politican. He'd started his political career a few years ago guesting on a local radio hate show called 'Freedom's Way,' hosted by a bilious racist named Paul Revere. This was his actual given name and he never let you forget it. I always pictured his audience as people sitting around in white sheets dousing huge crosses with gasoline in preparation for the night ahead. Burkhart became a legend on that program and, because of that, when the country was confused and enraged over Wall Street billionaires and endless charges of bank fraud, he recognized that this was the time for fanatics. He had a great presence, was a good speaker, and for all his average-guy hoo-hah was a bright, savvy man. In private he was said to frequently quote Ayn Rand. This wouldn't do when he was addressing the little people whom Rand scorned so much. They might think he was, you know, unmanly.

'We need to go,' I said, 'I can't take it anymore.'

TWO

I didn't want to be in Atherton and I particularly didn't want to be working with Congressman Jeff Ward. But four days earlier, when I'd been fighting my own client's battles, Tom Ward called me. After serving four terms in the House, my father had gone into the political consulting business. Tom Ward had been his best friend and most trusted employee.

Ward had also saved my father's life. In a scene out of the movie *Duel,* an eighteen-wheeler ran them off a narrow road in hilly country. They ended up in a fast, cold river. My father was knocked unconscious. Rather than save only himself, Tom swam my father to safety.

Years later he gave a moving speech at my father's funeral, one of those personal tributes that are by turns sad and funny and authentic. I'd known him since my teenage years and liked and trusted him as much as my father had.

'My son's in some trouble downstate, Dev. He's up against a man named Burkhart, one of those guys who wants to dismantle the federal government since the White House has been eternally sullied by a man of the colored persuasion. All the usual lies about Obama. As you probably know, Jeff's served two terms and this one should be a cinch for him, too, but it's anti-incumbency straight across the board. A very tough election cycle.

'Now I'm going to say some things about my son that may make it sound as if I don't love him, but that's not true. I love him very much. But you know what it's like growing up with an op for an old man. He's never home – I was never home – and the kids get raised by their mother. Jeff's an only child and Helen spoiled him rotten. And it doesn't help that he got *her* looks. He's got a rep as an ass bandit and unfortunately it's true. He can also be arrogant and nasty when the mood moves him. But he thinks right. Straight down the line he's for all the things we believe in. I'll give him that. He stands up when it matters. He's one of the few liberals who have no apologies to make. You've never met him, have you?'

'Just briefly.'

'Well, he's got a spy somewhere in his campaign and he won't admit it or deal with it. He keeps telling me that he'd know if he had a spy. He has a friend in the CIA so now he thinks he knows all about spying. But I know better. And I have to ask you if you'll go down there and check out his staff yourself. Just for a couple of days.'

'Tom, I'm facing my own problems here in Madison. We should be running eight, nine points ahead. I just saw some new internals this morning. We're four points ahead at best.'

'I know, Dev. But he's my kid.'

After my years with army intelligence, I started my own political consulting agency using many of the same methods my father had developed during his long tenure in the same business. Now I had a home office in Chicago with several employees and I still felt that the most useful things I'd learned were from my old man.

I thought of how moved my family was by Tom's words the morning of my father's funeral. I thought of how he and my dad used to laugh after work in the conference room with a six-pack of cold beer on the table between them. 'Two days max and I'm out.' I thought of how he'd saved my father's life.

'I'd do this myself, Dev, but when I offered he got really pissed. In fact, I have to warn you. He might even give you a little shit. Just tell him to buzz off. He resents any kind of outside help. He's got this little group around him and that's all he wants. I'm going to call him now and tell him you're coming. I'm also going to remind him that I brought him his biggest contributor. That'll shut him up for a while.'

After we hung up I thought through everything I'd heard about Jeff Ward. Bright, arrogant, combative, and rumored to have slept with a good share of Washington's finest available ladies – some married, some not. Somehow I'd never heard a word about a divorce. Maybe he had his wife bound and gagged in the basement.

I'm in no position to make moral judgments but I am in a position to avoid vortexes. You start to work for a client who has numerous sexual secrets, straight or gay doesn't matter, and you find yourself spending as much time suppressing the secrets as working on the election. Bill Clinton had a small army dealing with his past transgressions. That's work for other consulting firms, not mine.

I spent an hour on my Mac laptop reading up on Jeff Ward's political history and the people around him. He was working with a company out of San Diego that most consultants had given up on a few years back. I wanted my own opposition people.

I called the Silberman-Penski agency in Chicago and asked for Matt Boyle. The agency was a five-star international investigative firm that had wisely created an Internet department eight years ago, long before most of its competitors realized how to use the new development. They not only had the right equipment, they had the right young men and women. My firm used them exclusively. If you farted in church in 1971, they would present you with witness testimony in less than ten hours.

'Hey, Mr Conrad.'

'I think we're up to ninety bucks by now.'

'Oh, right. I forgot. Hey, Dev, how's it going?'

Matt and his wife Amy had both graduated at the top of their class at MIT. They were both deep-sea divers and mountain climbers. They loved adventure. And that included the adventure of being online detectives. If that involved hacking, I didn't know. I didn't want to know.

When I called and gave them a name, they knew what I was after. The kind of detail that can make a man think twice about staying in the race.

'The name is Rusty Burkhart. I checked. There's a fairly long story about him on Wikipedia. Can you start right away?'

'If I can't, Amy can.'

'Great. You've got my cell number.'

'You got it, Dev. Let's hope he's a serial killer.'

Jeff Ward was campaigning in the western section of his voting district when I'd flown into town last night so I'd yet to see him. His headquarters was one of those big, empty buildings that had housed a giant audio store before the economy committed suicide. Now it was the realm of phones, faxes, computers, stacks of campaign literature and posters of a handsome Irish man of thirty-six who liked to be depicted as a runner, a scrub basketball player, a swimmer and a man right at home in his district's only slum. The young black kids didn't look quite as taken with him as he might have hoped.

The private offices were on the second floor. Lucy found me a tiny room that had a phone and a small table for my laptop. I spent most of the first hour after seeing Burkhart checking with my people in Madison then with the people in Chicago. This cycle we had four clients up for re-election, including Ward.

I did more work on my Mac. I could see why Tom was convinced there was a spy in Ward's campaign. Ward and his four most important staffers would have a meeting to decide which theme to push in their next TV and radio campaign. Before they could get their advertising agency to get on the air with it, Burkhart would trump them with his own spot about the same theme. His own angle on it, of course. This always made it appear as if the Ward spots were responses to the Burkhart commercials. In other words, Ward always looked to be on the defensive. Once could be a coincidence. Even twice. But this had happened four times in a month. One of the staffers was on the Burkhart payroll.

I read the backgrounds Tom had sent me on the staffers. Nothing jumped out at me. These days we're a nation of narrow specialists and the political industry is no different. Each staffer had gone to a good state school; each had graduated with a BA in political science with minors in communications or sociology. Two had gone on to get graduate degrees. Each had started young with our party, spending high school time ringing doorbells and handing out literature and working as volunteers during their college years. They loved politics. It can be heartbreaking but it can also be exhilarating. And it's a job that matters. Congress is filled with people who shouldn't be there and I include a good number on our side. Vigilance is the key.

The meeting room was down the hall from me. Lucy said they tried to meet every day at four o'clock. I wandered down there.

The table was old and cigarette-scarred and chipped. Same for the chairs. On a far wall was a giant plasma TV screen. A gallery of Jeff Ward posters covered all the other available wall space. These were more somber than the ones downstairs. Here he was with his gorgeous wife and their two very beautiful little girls. Here he was in front of a cathedral with hard hats of different ethnicities standing around him. Two for one – God and the labor force. And here he was ladling out soup in a soup kitchen. He looked comfortable in the long white apron.

Lucy sat across the table from a young man in an inexpensive brown suit that was about the same color as his thinning hair. When he heard me come in he looked up and frowned.

'Jim Waters, say hello to Dev Conrad.'

He muttered something that might or might not have been hello.

'I think you can do a little better than that.'

He said, 'You're not here to fire me, are you?'

He was older than I'd thought at first, headed toward thirty. The eyes had the sadness and desperation of the outsider; not the rebellious outsider who taunted but the outsider who suffered. I had a cousin I'd been close to growing up much like that. He was and is a good man whom God or genes cast out in the darkness a long time ago and he hasn't been let back in since.

'Not at all, Jim, if I may call you that. I'm just here to check on a couple of things. Nothing about employment at all.'

He had a young, round face. His displeasure made him look petulant. 'I just don't like people coming in and telling me what I've been doing wrong. I've been writing speeches for seven years. I'm not exactly a beginner.'

If he was a dog he'd piss on the floor to mark his territory. That is always the danger of coming into a functioning campaign. They don't like you, heed you, or trust you. I'd feel the same way. Nobody wants to be second-guessed.

I leaned across the table and offered my hand. He stared at it as if he wasn't quite sure what it was, then he pouted a bit and finally shoved his hand into mine.

'Good to meet you, Jim. Let's get one thing straight, all right? The reason I'm here has absolutely nothing to do with anybody's job performance or anything like that. I'm just here to check out a couple of things with the congressman. I'm sure you don't believe that but it's the truth.'

He didn't look happy but at least he wasn't scowling any longer. 'I was sort of an asshole there. I apologize.'

'Thank you, Jim,' Lucy said. 'I just want him to meet the staff. Me included. If he was some kind of hired gun or something like that, my job would be on the line, too. And it isn't. And nobody else's is, either. We're hoping that Dev might have an idea or two for going up against Burkhart in the debate. That's one of Dev's specialties. Debates. He's handled several big ones.'

Waters was on his feet and headed for an automatic coffeemaker on a stand a few feet from the TV screen. 'You like yours black, Dev?' I had to get used to the quick change of tone. He sounded friendly now.

'That'd be great, Jim. I appreciate it.'

There was a woman's sweet laughter in the hall and two other people now appeared. This would be, according to Tom's back-grounder, Kathy Tomlin and David Nolan. Tomlin was the media coordinator and Nolan was Ward's chief of staff. Tomlin wore a green fitted dress and had a freckled face that was more pretty than beautiful. Nolan was tall, thin, wore wide red suspenders and, with his graying hair and rimless glasses, reminded me of many of my professors in college. He was the opposite of his lifelong friend the congressman. Jeff Ward was a taker with an almost piratical swagger. His number one staffer – and some said the authentic thinker of the duo – was a giver. Though they were the same age, Nolan looked fifteen years older than Ward.

He also looked distracted. He sat down now, glanced around, then opened the laptop he'd set on the table. He immediately began staring at some presumably compelling image the rest of us couldn't see. He'd either been crying recently or was miserably hung-over. His gaze belonged on a homeless man.

Kathy Tomlin said, 'I don't really have much today. I'm sorry. The only news – and so far it's only scuttlebutt – is that some far-right organization is going to give Burkhart a million dollars' worth of commercials they're putting together. These are the creeps who brought down Helen Agee two years ago. The good old lesbian smear. It was ridiculous but they made it work. But fortunately David's got some ideas to help us.'

She finished, sounding expectant. Nolan would pick up her cue and take it from there. But he didn't. He was still staring off into the distance. Apparently he could no longer endure staring at the screen.

'David,' Kathy repeated softly.

'Oh.' He looked neither flustered nor embarrassed. He just seemed confused. 'Oh, right.' He sat up straight in his chair. Lucy and Waters studied him. I wasn't the only one puzzled by his behavior. 'Right.' He tried a smile that was more a grimace. Then he turned in my direction. 'You must be Dev Conrad.'

'That's right.'

'Jeff's father has a lot of faith in you. I hope you can help us.' His eyes weren't quite focused. And then he stopped talking. I wondered if he was physically sick. His face gleamed with sweat. 'What was I saying, Kathy?'

'The right-wing contributions for Burkhart.'

'Oh, yes, right.' His attempt at a smile was embarrassing. Around the table the eyes studied him with silent alarm. He settled back in his chair, as if he was relaxed now. In control of himself again. But when he began to speak it was obvious he'd either forgotten or chose not to talk about the right-wing group Kathy had talked about.

I wondered if he'd had a stroke. His behavior certainly suggested that. I wasn't alone. The three staffers looked at each other anxiously.

He reached for a silver pitcher of water to fill the glass in front of him. His hand was trembling so badly he dropped the pitcher almost as soon as he started to raise it. It landed hard. Though it was in no danger of spilling, the staffers automatically started to rise in their chairs to grab it.

'Oh, God,' Lucy half whispered. 'David, are you—?'

'What was I saying?' Nolan said as if he was unaware of his strange behavior. 'Oh – right. Well, I contacted this group of investors who frankly think it's time to do a little business with our side. They know everything's up for grabs in this election but they still think it's time to have a sit-down with somebody we know in the administration. They're willing to spend thirty million dollars on making and airing some generic commercials that favor us. They won't spend it all on our district; they want to make it as national as possible.' He stopped talking. An engine that had run down.

'What makes this so interesting,' Kathy said quickly, 'aside from the money is that three of the products they want some federal funding for – they need further research – are very eco-friendly. That means the other party doesn't want anything to do with them. Unfortunately, a lot of our senators and reps are on the same payroll and will vote against us. But I think we've still got enough votes. And David thinks so, too, don't you?'

The smile that was a grimace again. Was he in pain? 'Right.' His eyes brightened. There was strength in his voice now. 'I'm hoping we get at least four million. We can put a lot of that into radio and some extra TV.'

Lucy and Waters did the power fist.

'I'll bet Jeff was happy when he heard about it,' Lucy said.

Nolan's jaw clenched. He said nothing.

'We haven't had a chance to tell him yet. But he'll be happy as hell. You can bet on it.' Kathy touched Nolan's arm and said, 'Good work, David.' She was a nurse talking to a very sick patient.

'Excellent work,' Lucy said in the same way.

The accolades didn't free him from whatever mental prison he was in. The smile was a little less pensive at their words but something troubled him so much that he was barely present.

'Well,' he said, pushing back from the table. 'Guess I should get back to work.'

Which made no sense. Wasn't this, what he was doing at the moment, work?

He next did a sight gag, getting his foot tangled in the legs of the chair as he stood up and tried to walk. He almost fell down, righting himself then muttering more to himself than us, 'I'm fine, I'm fine.' Then he glanced at me. 'I'm glad you're here, Dev. We need you to help with the debate. It's make or break for us.'

'Is he all right?' Lucy asked Kathy when he was gone.

'I think so.' She didn't sound sure. 'I think maybe the hours he puts in are finally catching up with him. I think he should take two days off and do nothing but rest and go for walks. He loves to walk.'

'He's usually the one who keeps all of us up and excited,' Lucy said to me. 'Maybe he really is just tired out.'

But she knew better than that and so did I.

Kathy glanced at me and frowned. 'This wasn't a very good introduction to our team here, Mr Conrad. I hope the rest of the day goes a lot smoother than this.'

'No sense hiding it, Kathy,' Waters said. 'We've had a lot of ups and downs lately. That's just the way it is.'

The two women looked uncomfortable but they said nothing.

I wondered if one of these three was the spy feeding information to Burkhart.

THREE

'He just looks so presidential,' one older woman said to another standing under the poster of Congressman Jeff Ward leaning back to throw a football à la John Kennedy. They seemed to be in their Sunday best, right down to small white gloves. They were the kind of women you always saw at weekday Mass. Decent people who'd worked hard for very little all their lives and whose grandparents and parents had indoctrinated them to vote for our party. There was something endearing about them, their old-fashioned coats and dresses and makeup and sweet perfume. They were out of their time and I liked that without quite knowing why. These are the kind of supporters who will bake cookies for fund drives and make arrangements for voters who need rides to the polls. They're invaluable.

Since high school had ended at least an hour ago, the head-quarters was also packed with teenagers receiving instructions about getting out posters, signs, pamphlets, and door-to-door reminders about the elections coming up. For all of TV's vaunted powers – and those powers are primary – you still need a ground attack, and that means volunteers who want to win as badly as the candidate does. And if you're sixteen or seventeen and male it means working on a campaign can get you in close proximity to girls – and I suspect it just might work the other way for girls – you might not otherwise meet. Romance was always in the air during campaigns.

The people working the ground floor were as efficient and functional as the people on the second floor seemed not to be. Middle-aged women and men of both blue collar and white sending the kids off to war with repeated orders and smiles.

I drifted back to where three coffeepots burbled. A white-haired woman in a small flowery apron was just setting out a tray of homemade cookies decorated with the word 'Ward' in red. 'Help yourself.'

'Thank you. I think I will.'

'That is, if you're planning to vote for Congressman Ward.'

'I would if he was in my district but I vote in Chicago.'

'Well, I guess that entitles you to a cookie, anyway. My name's Joan Rosenberg. I run the kitchen back there.'

'You're obviously doing a great job.'

'They'll be gone in less than twenty minutes. And that'll make me very happy.' A wry smile. 'On one campaign I worked on a long time ago back in the sixties, the only people who'd eat my cookies were the ones who smoked marijuana. I think the older people were thinking I put some pot in my cookies. My husband's a rabbi. He sure didn't want people to think his wife was making illegal cookies.' She laughed. 'I'd be on *America's Most Wanted.*'

It was nice to bask in her goodwill and intelligence. Not to mention her lack of cunning. A gentle, sweet woman of the kind who always turns out for campaigns. They have ideals and support them with hard work. And none of the cynicism of the professionals rubs off on them.

I followed her eyes to the door that led to the back. Jim Waters was making his way toward us.

'Hi, Jim. They're just out of the oven.' She pointed to the cookies.

By now I'd had my first bite. I held it up as if I was in a commercial. 'This is terrific.'

I noticed that she put her hand on Waters' shoulder as he bent to whisk a cookie from the plate. I also noticed that the merriment in her brown eyes changed to concern. She looked maternal watching him, patting him a few times as he straightened up.

As he took his first taste he said, 'You never miss, Joan. This is great.' But despite his words the round face, not quite adult but not quite teenager either, sagged into an expression of hurt, maybe even loss. I'd focused on his anger upstairs. Now I saw what was behind the anger.

'How're you doing today, Jim? Better than yesterday?'

These two had a history. She wanted to be brought up to date. Obviously she'd been thinking about him.

'Yeah. A little better, I guess.'

He glanced at me. I realized I was in the way. I finished my cookie and grabbed my paper cup of coffee. 'Guess I'll wander back up front. Thanks very much for the cookie.' I nodded to Waters. 'Maybe we should have dinner tonight if you've got time.'

He looked surprised, then suspicious. 'Yeah, maybe.'

Up front several teenagers were trying to hang a large WARD. FOR THE PEOPLE. sign that would stretch from one side of the large room to the other. They were having a good time, especially the couples who were flirting and joking.

I walked up to the front window and looked out at the street. People were starting to drive home from work. Traffic clogged the four-lane avenue. As the front door opened and closed I could smell autumn again and it made me wonder what my college senior daughter was doing. Unlike me she was a sports fan. She loved football games especially. She never wanted for dates to games or any kind of social events, not only having inherited her mother's brains but also her good looks. Then I thought of what Tom Ward said about how consultants make less than ideal fathers. Even though she'd lived with her mother except for the month she spent with me every summer, she loved me enough to forgive me and we were now not only father and daughter but true friends.

Then a voice said, 'I'll take you up on that dinner, Dev. And I won't be such a shit.' Even his grin was glum. 'You just kind of scared me, I guess.'

'I'm pretty harmless, Jim. Nobody's going to lose his or her job.'

He tried to make a joke of it. 'Well, I'm too important to fire, right? A big shot like me?'

'You're probably right. I read some of the recent speeches you wrote for Ward. They're excellent.'

'Oh, hell, they weren't anything special.' He waved my words away, looking uncomfortable. 'I wrote better ones last year.'

I gave him my card. 'I'll be eating at the hotel tonight. Just give me a call.'

'I will. I – I've got some things we need to talk about.' Another awkward look, and then he swung around and headed quick and dead-on to the door.

As he left I got another scent of Halloween season. Then I happened to notice the blonde in the silver Porsche. She was almost directly across from me so I got a good look at her face. She was one of those fashionable country club women, all blonde and sculpted and self-reverent, like a sexual icon you could admire but never know. Just now she raised a camera with a long lens to her face and began snapping away. Since Waters was the only person on the street and since her lens moved with him as he walked, there was no doubt he was her subject.

She adjusted the lens once then put the camera down. Half a minute later she shot out of her parking space and bulleted into traffic. I'd already written the license number down.

Who would be following Waters to photograph him? I felt pretty certain she wasn't federal or local law. I also felt certain that he was in trouble of some kind.

'Ready for another cookie?'

I had to pry my gaze from the street. What the hell was going on? 'Don't mind if I do.' I pointed to the nearly empty pan. 'You're beating your best time. It's been about ten minutes and they're almost gone.'

'As I said, that makes me happy. I'm an empty nester. We had three kids and they're all grown and gone now. This brings them back. Sort of.'

I took a bite. I hoped the hotel food was this good. 'Did Jim talk about me?'

'Yes.' Her brow tightened. 'He's afraid you'll get him fired. I hope that's not true.'

'It isn't. Not in any way.'

She sighed and mimed fanning herself. 'Whoosh. Good. I've gotten to know him over the past month and a half. I just feel sorry for him. He lost his brother in a boating accident three years ago, he told me. But I'm sure it goes back before that. He's the nerdy boy who tells you how superior he is every once in a while. You know, being defensive. I've seen him once or twice try to come on to women around here and it's painful to watch. People are so cruel to him and he doesn't know how to defend himself. He's so down on himself and people sense that and they make jokes about him. A lot of the time to his face.'

'Has he ever said anything to you about being in trouble?'

She set the last three cookies on a plate then picked up the metal sheet she'd baked them on. 'That's a strange question.' She now took the time to examine me. 'I don't know if I should be talking about anything . . . private.'

'I've spent a little time with him and noticed that he seems worried about something. Innocent question. My name's Dev Conrad, by the way. I'm working with the campaign for a few days.'

She stood the cookie sheet on its end and set her hands on it.
'He had tears in his eyes the other day. I asked him what was wrong.
And I thought it was funny because he wouldn't tell me. He just
shrugged and said maybe it would all work out. He usually tells
me everything. Or at least that was the impression I had. He might
have been holding a lot back from me all this time. I can't be sure.
But whatever this was it made him very upset. I'd never seen him
quite that way, really depressed. Later I saw him up at the front
window, staring out at the street. I walked up to him. He jerked
away from me. I'd really scared him. I felt sorry for embarrassing
him because people started looking at him. I know he was mad at
me for a few minutes so I walked away. I really felt that I'd betrayed
him in some way.'

The street. The Porsche. Being followed. So he'd been aware of
it. Would he bolt if I brought up any of this tonight over dinner?
There was definitely a spy in the campaign. I wasn't sure what he
was involved in but I wouldn't be surprised if he was the man I
was looking for.

'Thanks very much, Joan.'

She held her cookie sheet in front of her like a shield. 'Just be
easy with him, Dev. He needs all the friends he can get.'

As I nodded and walked away, I wondered if he had any special
friends in the Burkhart camp.

FOUR

There was a café in the hotel where I was staying. Before going up to my room I decided to have another cup of coffee. I'm one of the lucky ones. I don't have any trouble taking a nap after a day's worth of regular coffee. And a nap was what I was planning.

The café was busy with people who had decided that the food here was what they wanted instead of the more dramatic feast awaiting them in the hotel restaurant. I found a copy of the day's *Chicago Tribune* and took one of the few empty booths.

Tuning out the clamor took a few minutes. Dishes clattering, waitresses calling out orders to the cooks, laughter, the occasional shout of 'We're over here!' and the hostess asking me if I was sure all I wanted was coffee. This was how she let me know that she didn't like the idea – not at all – that I was taking up a booth for a lousy two-dollar cup of coffee. It wasn't worth explaining that I would have been happy to sit at the counter but all the stools were taken.

The *Trib* did an extensive rundown of state races. According to their numbers we were only four points behind Burkhart. They noted that we'd been down but were struggling back now. This was the best kind of press and I hoped the local TV news people would pick it up. As much as they liked Burkhart, they liked the horse race even more. This was the kind of story they could lead with, even though public polls generally aren't as reliable as our own internals.

The other story that interested me was about a Montana man who'd announced for governor saying that there were some who thought that this country would be better off if we tried the president for treason. It was too easy to claim, as too many Beltway media stars insisted, that what we were experiencing was just a silly season of nut jobs. But as I'd seen this afternoon, handguns and assault weapons made this season anything but silly. Insurrection was in the air. People came close to saying that the president should be murdered. And by now there was enough such talk that the mainstream media took it all in their stride.

'You look angry.'

I raised my head to stare into the ice-blue eyes of Kathy Tomlin, Jeff Ward's media buyer.

'Not any more so than usual.' She was nice enough to match my smile.

'Mind if I sit down?'

'Not at all.'

I've learned that when a pretty girl, and by God she was, offers to sit with you, the idea of turning her away rarely crosses your mind. She was a bit tousled and worn from the day but that only meant she worked hard and took things seriously.

'I'm almost afraid to ask you what you thought of our staff. We're all a little wasted.'

'I've seen worse.'

'That bad?'

'Are you kidding? I once spent three days with a staff that had fist fights right in the office. The campaign manager got his nose smashed in the last day I was there. And three of the women were planning on filing sexual harassment suits.'

'Wow. Could you give me their address? That sounds like fun.' Very white teeth. You could fall in love with those teeth.

'They've disbanded. The campaign manager went to the slammer for embezzling, one of the single girls got pregnant, two of the married women got divorced and one of the tough guys got punched out by a guy half his size.'

'They were all on our side, of course.'

'Of course.'

This time the smile was wan. 'I used to be so idealistic.'

'My father was a political consultant for most of his life. Jeff's father saved his life, in fact. They worked together. I've always had the fever but I lost the idealism by the time I was fifteen or so.'

'Your virginity.'

'In a way, I suppose.'

A waitress hovered. Kathy ordered. She had just made the hostess happy. The booth was now occupied by at least one person who was ordering food. 'They have the best cheeseburgers in town. That's why I always come here after work. Especially nights when I have to go back to the office. My little treat.'

I sat back. 'What's wrong with Nolan?'

'That's a strange question.'

'He was there in body only today. One minute he looked sad, the next he looked like he was having an out-of-body experience.'

'I'm sure he's just worn out like the rest of us. We've worked so hard. We planned on being six or seven points up by now. David was the only one who kept saying we weren't taking Burkhart seriously enough. Jeff just laughed him off, said he was a freak. Turns out David was right. As usual.'

'So you don't know of any major personal problem he's having?'

I had the sense she was holding something back from me. 'No, no. He's just a very serious guy. He works very hard mentally and sometimes he's just off in his own little world. You aren't eating?'

The transition closed off further questions. 'I need to catch some sleep. I've had about four hours in the last thirty hours and it's starting to take its toll. I'm supposed to look things over and see if I can come up with any ideas for improvement.'

'So you're really not going to suggest firing people?'

'Yes, I am. And I'm thinking of starting with you.'

She said, 'I think you like me. I don't think you'd do it.'

'I'd like you even more if I wasn't falling asleep.'

'I must be fascinating company.'

I stood up. 'I think you know better than that.'

The dreams I had disturbed me. When the call came on my cell phone I had to claw my way through the afterbirth of the people and images I'd created. In that instant when I was free again I felt depressed, even a bit afraid.

Lucy Cummings was half shouting. 'You need to get down here right away.'

'Lucy?'

'Oh God, Dev. Were you asleep? I'm sorry. The police are here and everything.'

'The police?'

'Somebody killed Jim Waters and left him in his car. I found him about half an hour ago.'

I almost said that Waters was supposed to have called me about dinner. But that was useless and pointless information now.

I was on my feet. 'Is Jeff there?'

'He was out at the local college for a talk tonight. But he canceled and rushed back here.'

'All right. I'll be there in a few minutes.'

In the bathroom I splashed water on my face. I kept thinking of the things Joan Rosenberg had told me about Waters. A lost soul for sure. I also thought about how he didn't fit into the group around Congressman Ward. They were sleek pros. He was an awkward loner without any polish at all.

I grabbed a fresh shirt and pair of chinos and then worked into my dark blue suede jacket. I felt sorry for Waters the more I played back some of the things he'd said and the way he'd looked. But those feelings only made me wonder about what he'd been going to tell me at dinner.

FIVE

E mergency lights of red and blue played across the night sky like tracers in a war. Traffic was down to one lane east and west. The crowd was already formidable. TV people lugging cameras and camera packs surged against the cops who pushed them back into the crowd.

I got as close as I could – three-quarters of a long block away – and tried to figure out which would be the fastest way to get to a cop. The night air was chill and fresh, that autumn briskness that can revive the dead. All too soon I was working my way with elbows and nudges through knots of people who'd gathered to be terrified and spellbound by death. Aromas of perfume, aftershave, cigarettes, sweat, booze.

I was pretty sure the last guy I squeezed by wanted to punch me but then he looked at my face. I was at least five inches taller than he was so he decided against it. I was never especially tough but I'd learned how to look and act tough without getting all John Wayne about it. (I read a piece of movie criticism lately that set forth the notion that John Wayne and Clint Eastwood were a boy's notion of what tough guys were whereas Lee Marvin was the real thing. I agreed.)

Even before I opened my mouth the uniformed woman standing sentry said, 'Get back in line there!'

I shoved my wallet at her.

'Am I supposed to be impressed?'

'I'm a consultant working with the Ward campaign. They called me at my hotel and told me to get over here right away.'

She flipped the wallet open. 'Dev Conrad.'

'That's right. You can check me out.'

She waved me back then went to work on her communicator. She turned away as she spoke. She was probably saying that there was this loser here who was trying to crash the crime scene. Then she was in my face again. 'They're checking you out. Just stay where you are.'

She started walking her side of the line. A male uniform worked the rest of it.

From the conversations around me nobody but the cops had any idea what had happened here. The word 'terrorist' sliced the air though I wasn't sure what that was supposed to mean. If a terrorist of some kind had killed Waters he must have been one of Burkhart's crazier followers.

Several feet away the female officer started talking to her shoulder again. She studied me as she listened. As she walked up to me she said, 'I guess you're all right. You can walk up to the front door and the sergeant there will tell you what to do then.' Her tone said she still didn't like me or trust me.

A half-dozen voices started whining behind me. They didn't know who I was but they sure as hell didn't like me anyway. I could have been a priest, rabbi, or even doctor. It didn't matter. I was some jerk-off who got to go inside.

The sergeant was a burly middle-aged black man with gray hair and gray mustache. He was at least as skeptical about me as the female cop had been. 'You belong in here, huh?'

'I'm working here for a few days.'

'This is a crime scene.'

I didn't say anything.

'That means you don't touch anything and I mean anything. You walk along that wall to the back where you'll ask for Lieutenant Neame. She's a lady. She'll take it from there.'

We stood just outside the entrance. He pointed to the wall I was to follow. 'I'm going to be standing here watching you. You go straight back and you make it fast. I got other problems I need to attend to.'

I shrugged and started my walk. I wasn't alone. Four cops with flashlights were scanning the ground looking for anything worth bagging.

Lieutenant Neame was big and dark-haired. I imagined she was something of an athlete. With her gray pantsuit and snappy voice she had the intimidation thing down just right. She dispatched her troops with blunt force trauma. God help you if you disobeyed. Part of this, I assumed, was for show. She needed to hold her own with all the macho guys who didn't like taking orders from a woman.

'And you would be Dev Conrad, I guess, huh?'

'That's what they tell me.'

'Cute.' Then: 'Did you know James Francis Waters?'

The back of the headquarters was filled with an ambulance and three squad cars. A dusty, dull, ten-year-old Volvo sat in the center of the parking lot. The hood and the trunk were up. All the doors were open. Three different officers in suits worked over the interior.

'I met him this afternoon. We were supposed to have dinner tonight.'

'What time?'

'We left that open. I went back to my hotel to have a nap. He had my cell phone number. He was supposed to call me. Then we were supposed to eat in the hotel restaurant.'

'That's the Royale?'

'Right.'

'Any special reason you were having dinner with him?'

Before I could answer, two of the cops working on the car came up to her. The three of them had one of those football-like huddles meant to exclude the ears of outlanders. Namely me.

When they were done she was all mine again. 'So why were you having dinner with him?'

'I'm just here for forty-eight hours. He was under the impression – the wrong impression – that I was here to suggest shaking up the staff.'

'Meaning firing people?'

'Right.'

'Just why *are* you here?'

'Every campaign needs to be assessed from time to time. Congressman Ward's father was a close friend of my father's. Tom Ward thought I might have a few ideas about improving things here. Streamlining them.'

'He's not going to win. Burkhart is.'

'Is that a paid political announcement?'

She was very good at hiding how much she cared for me.

'Ward and three of his staffers are inside being interviewed by two of my officers. I want them to interview you, too.'

'I don't know much. I didn't meet the staff until a few hours ago.'

'The back door is standing open. Don't touch anything or speak to any of the officers. They're busy. Just go straight inside. One of the officers in uniform will take you to where the interviews are being conducted. This place is going to be hell within another twenty minutes or so. We need you all to cooperate because we're going to get state press here right away. And maybe even national press, too. And that's going to make our job one hell of a lot harder.'

'I understand.'

The downturn of her lips said she doubted it.

She was right about the uniformed officer waiting for me just inside the opened back door. He was young, tall, scrawny, and had an Adam's apple the size of a baseball.

'Follow me, please.'

The police were using the conference room for the interviews. Two offices down sat Lucy Cummings and Kathy Tomlin.

The officer escorted me inside the office and then pointed to the sole empty chair on the visitor's side of the desk. Nobody said anything. I sat down next to Lucy.

'He's dead,' Kathy said. Big tears loomed on the lower edges of her blue eyes. 'At least he died in that Captain America jacket he loved so much. It sounds crazy, but it meant a lot to him.' Then: 'I wish I would have been more of a help to him.'

Enough of remorse. There would be time for that later. The big problem now was managing the press. 'What the hell happened, anyway?' All I knew was that he'd been found murdered in his car. This would be the most predictable kind of story – a mystery inside a political campaign. Was some sleazy secret being kept from the public? Was this poor young man killed because he knew too much? Burkhart would hire extra PR flacks to push this story twenty-four/seven.

Lucy hid her face in her hands. Her shoulders shook. I slid my arm around her.

Kathy said, 'I'd be the same way Lucy is if I'd found him, Dev. She told me she heard two noises that she thought might be gunshots. She ran to the back door to look through the window. She saw Jim's car back there. The door was open and she could see a foot dangling beneath it.'

Lucy took her hands from her face and with a great deal of sniffling and snuffling said, 'I ran out there. It was stupid because whoever'd fired the gun might still be out there. But I knew something had happened to Jim. And that's how I found him. He'd been shot in the side of the head. Poor Jimmy.' The face went into the hands again. The shoulders shook once more.

Kathy finished the story. 'She told me she saw the blood on the side of his head. Where the bullet had gone in. And then somehow she managed to call 911 on her cell phone. When I came in I heard her throwing up in the bathroom. I went in and she managed to tell me about Jim. By then the police were here.'

'What about enemies?' I said. 'Did he ever mention somebody being after him or something?'

'No,' Kathy said. 'Though we got a lot of threats on the phone and in the mail. Not so much here. But in Jeff's congressional office across town – you know, where people can come to get help. They've had to close down twice because they found things that looked like they might be bombs. And one night somebody spray-painted 'Nigger Lover' on their front window. And 'Death to Tyrants.' You know, because of Obama. Things like that got to all of us. I got to the point where I'd park as close to the back door here as I could so at night I didn't have to walk far to get in my car and go home. All these guns floating around and all these threats scared everybody. Campaigns always get rough but we've never seen anything like this. It affected everybody.'

'The police will have to look into the possibility that he was robbed.'

'Jim didn't have any money to speak of,' Kathy said.

'These days you can get killed for fifty cents,' I said. 'Right now that's a possibility we have to consider.'

'So it could be just a coincidence?' Lucy sniffled.

'Possibly,' I said. 'It's not out of the question. But what I'm worried about is how the press is going to handle this.'

Kathy nodded. 'Burkhart's already put out a lot of brochures playing up Jeff's reputation as an ass bandit. He managed to dig up all these old photos of when Jeff was still single and dressing up in dinner jackets and going out with great-looking young women on his arm. Before he was married, Jeff used to date this beautiful black woman. Naturally that's the biggest photo in all the brochures and handouts.'

'Where did Jim live?' I asked.

Kathy scribbled the address on a piece of paper and handed it to me. She also gave me directions.

'But won't the police be there now?' Kathy said.

'Not if I get there first.'

'The police will want to talk to you.'

And they did. When I reached the bottom of the stairs, a slender man with red hair and a red mustache held up a hand to stop me. 'I'm Detective Fincher. Did any of our people interview you upstairs?'

'No. I was in kind of a hurry. There were two officers and they were busy interviewing other people so I just left.'

'You could be in some trouble leaving like that. What's your name?'

'Dev Conrad.'

From the pocket of his gray tweed sport coat he took a small notebook. He flipped open the cover and then clicked the ballpoint pen so that it was ready for action. 'And you work for Congressman Ward?'

'I'm a consultant Congressman Ward hired. I just got here last night. My first full day with the campaign. I met Jim Waters briefly. We were supposed to get together later tonight for dinner.'

'Any particular reason?'

We had to keep shifting positions to let law enforcement people in and out of the back door.

'We'd gotten off to a bad start. Whenever campaigns bring in a new consultant the staff get nervous. Start thinking they might get fired. I'd be the same way. He said a few things and then apologized for them a little later. No big deal. I just thought it'd be a good thing to agree to meet him. Smooth things over. He seemed to want to talk.'

'About what?'

'I never found out.'

The alley was filling up with press-fighting uniformed officers bent on keeping them away from the car where Waters had been killed. Fincher glanced at the struggle and frowned. The press was not necessarily beloved where he worked.

'So you wouldn't have any idea why he was killed tonight?'

'None. I really didn't know him.'

He glanced at the surging reporters again. 'They'd destroy the crime scene if you gave them half a chance.' Then: 'Where're you headed now?'

I could've told him that he had no right to ask me that question but I was in a hurry. I wanted to check out Waters' apartment before the police did. I wanted to take away anything that might embarrass the campaign. Drugs, S&M gear, unexplained stacks of money. You just never knew what you'd find. And cops talk. Anything salacious they found would be on TV within hours of the police searching Waters' place.

'Believe it or not, I'm going back to my hotel room to get some sleep.'

'We'll want to ask you more questions, I'm sure. You got a card?'

I extracted one from my billfold and gave it to him. 'I'm staying at the Royale.'

He didn't even look at it, just tucked it between the pages of his notebook. 'Somebody from the station will be contacting you.'

I nodded and started off in the direction of my rental. I had to restrain myself from breaking into a run. I needed to go through Waters' apartment and I didn't have much time.

The Carlton Arms had been new probably sometime in the early sixties. The tan color and texture of the brick facing dated back to that era. But neither time nor its residents had been kind to it. The asphalt parking lot had ridges where heat and cold had split it. A number of the windows on the west side had been smashed and were covered with cardboard and tape. Music ranging from rap to country-western boomed and screeched from various apartments.

I didn't see any police vehicles, marked or not, so I pulled in and walked up to the glass door with SECTION B neatly painted above it. It wouldn't be long before the officials arrived.

I knocked on the door marked *Manager. Pierce Rollins*. Except for Pierce Brosnan I'd never heard of a man with that first name.

The guy who opened the door was not my idea of a 'Pierce.' He was probably in his mid-twenties. He had a wicked devil-style beard and arms that had been covered with a tattoo artist's fiercest supernatural creatures.

'It's a little late, buddy.' Behind him was a somewhat overweight but attractive woman in a black chemise smoking a cigarette. I guess she hadn't read the No Smoking sign that greeted folks when they came through the front door.

'Jim Waters called me – he wants me to pick up something for him.'

He was suddenly interested enough to look at me seriously. The
TV set went crazy with laughter. The woman laughed, too. 'You're
missing this, babe.'

'You'd be who?'

I showed him my identification. 'I work with the campaign. I'm
just here for a couple of days. We're out at a rally on the edge of
town. Jim wanted to call you but we're in a valley out there and
his cell won't work.'

The woman laughed again and said, 'C'mon, babe. You'd love
this.'

'Why bother me with this shit? He must've given you a key. He's
on the second floor in Apartment D. Handle it yourself.'

'Just thought I'd touch base.'

'Yeah. Touch base. Shit.'

The way he slammed the door, he must have awakened more
than half his tenants.

The smells of various dinners collided just the way the disparate
music had. Spaghetti, some kind of fish, burgers. The hall carpeting
had cuts and holes in it. On the tan walls you could see where dirty
words had almost been scrubbed out. I'd checked in with the manager
in case he got a complaint that I was seen unlocking Jim Waters'
door. I didn't have a key; I had the three burglar picks I'd kept from
my days as an army investigator.

Captain America was going to kick my ass. That was the sense
I had anyway as soon as I flipped on the living-room light of this
one-bedroom apartment. The poster covered half the wall facing
me. He looked very, very pissed and as you well know, nobody
fucks with the Captain.

There were other posters, too. Two quite comely and mostly
naked starlets whose names I didn't know. Then a small gallery, on
another wall, of terrifying comic book figures. Creatures that resembled humans but were in fact ghouls of some kind carrying axes,
enormous knives, bludgeons, and severed heads. All of them dripped
blood and all of them walked over bloody arms and legs and faces.

Real life hadn't been kind to Jim and so he'd retreated into fantasy
life here where he was not only safe but accepted. I heard echoes
of Lucy Cummings crying and felt some of her sadness. He'd been
aggrieved by so many things.

No idea what I was looking for, I tried to log on to his computer but it was password protected, and the small table he used for a desk in the corner held nothing more than a Brother printer and blank paper.

In his bedroom I found more posters plus five long cardboard boxes jammed tight with comic books. They'd been sorted and catalogued. The drawers of his dresser were sparsely filled with socks with holes and underwear that had outlived its shelf life. Under one small pile of undershirts I found three bullets for a .38. I wondered where the gun was. I went through the three-shelf bookcase next to his mussed bed. Robert Jordan and R.A. Salvatore and *Star Wars* tie-ins outnumbered all the other authors represented.

The closet was filled with clothes that must have dated back to his college days; maybe high school, some of them. He'd never been stylish.

Coats often held interesting items so I started on them. A cheap blue trench coat didn't produce anything, nor did a Fighting Illini jacket or any of the other clothing.

'I'll bring the key back when I'm done, Pierce.'

Voice. Young. Female. Shouting down the steps.

A key rasped in the lock.

I was standing in the center of the room when the door opened and she appeared.

The style is called Goth. This young woman was in a fitted black dress with black tights, dyed black hair, and black lipstick. She was no more than twenty years old and hard as she tried she couldn't disguise the fact that she was quite pretty in a somewhat waifish way.

'Who the hell are you, mister?'

'I could ask you the same thing.'

'I'm Jimmy's collaborator.'

'On what?'

'On none of your fucking business.'

I couldn't help it. I smiled.

'What's so funny, smart ass?'

'Nothing's funny, believe me. You're just so damn belligerent and for no reason. You'd better come in. We need to talk.'

'You still haven't told me who you are.'

'My name's Dev Conrad.'

She walked past me with great disdain. She pitched her purse on the couch then opened it up to rescue her cigarettes and lighter. After she sat down she said, 'Where's Jimmy?'

'Jimmy's dead. Somebody murdered him a couple of hours ago.'

She took at least half a minute to respond. There was no gasping, no sobbing, no clasping her hand to her breast. The only evidence that she'd been stunned by what I said was the tremor in the fingers that held the cigarette.

'Oh, my God. So Rachel was right.'

'What?'

Her grave blue eyes met mine. 'Rachel McClure. She's a friend of mine. She can see the future.'

'I see.'

'Don't give me any of your 'I see' bullshit. If I tell you she can see the future, she can see the future, all right?' Her voice had risen to just below a scream.

'All right.'

'And she was getting these vibes about Jimmy. She didn't want to tell him because that would just freak him out. Jimmy is very sensitive.'

'When's the last time you saw Jimmy?'

'Two nights ago. If it's any of your business.' She crossed her legs. Then uncrossed them. Then crossed them again. 'What the hell are you staring at?'

'You. I just want to make sure you're all right.'

'Oh, I see. Maybe you want to come over here and sit next to me. Maybe slide your arm around me. Maybe grab a cheap feel. Something like that?'

'I like women a little older.'

'What, eighty or ninety?'

'That's a nice range.'

She sort of flounced in place. Then threw her head back and stared at the ceiling. She had a classic neck. 'He's dead; Jimmy's dead. Jimmy's fucking dead. No way I can believe this.' Her head snapped back into its normal position and she glared at me. 'You're not making this up, are you?'

'Why would I make it up?'

'Oh, I don't know. Maybe because I walk in here and find you doing God-knows-what to his apartment. How do I know you're not some robber?'

'Exactly what would I take from this place? His Captain America poster?'

'You making fun of Jimmy, you bastard?'

'No. I'm just pointing out that there isn't anything in here that would have much resale value.' Then: 'How old are you?'

'Not old enough to interest you. Thank God.'

'C'mon. How old?'

'Nineteen. Wanna see my license?'

'Yeah.'

She flung her purse at me. I opened it and lifted her wallet free. The license read Jennifer Kelly Conners. Her Goth photo was ominous. She had to have worked hard to get it that way. Her age was listed as nineteen. I dropped wallet back into purse and sent purse sailing through the air to couch.

'Jimmy keep any liquor here?'

'You gonna drink his booze?'

'I'm not. You are. So where is it?'

'There's beer in the fridge and a bottle of Jack Daniel's black in the cupboard. I gave it to him for his birthday but he hasn't ever opened it. He likes beer.'

I found the Jack and poured a shot into a *Transformers* glass that was a promotional item when the second film came out. I brought the glass to her then took the tattered armchair across from her.

'You think this is going to make me tell you all his secrets?'

'Something like that.'

'Well, you'd have to do a hell of a lot better than this.' To prove it she knocked it off in a single gulp.

'I'm impressed.'

'Screw you.'

'So what were Jimmy's secrets?'

She had a wild, somewhat deranged laugh. 'God, you're too much of a dork to be a robber.'

'Thank you. By the way, why did you borrow Pierce's key and come in here?'

'Because I used to have a key of my own but I lost it in some club. Jimmy loved to come home and find me waiting for him. And anyway, who the hell are you?'

I explained why I was in town and that I was supposed to have met Jimmy tonight for dinner. Then I gussied up the reason for the dinner. 'He said there was something he needed to tell me. Something he was worried about. My impression was that he was afraid about something.'

She dropped her cigarette into the glass I'd given her. The fiery end of it sizzled. 'If you're asking me what he was afraid of I couldn't tell you.'

'But you knew he was afraid.'

'I suppose I did.'

'Did he ever give you a clue about anything?'

She rolled the glass back and forth in her black-nailed fingers. 'He said he was going to have enough money to take off to Europe and maybe get lost over there. Which pissed me off.'

'Why would that piss you off?'

'Hello – have you been listening to me? We were supposed to be collaborators. How could we be collaborators if he was in Europe?'

'I see.'

'I also pointed out to him that every time he talked about the money he'd get real nervous. His voice would go up an octave. And sometimes he'd stutter a few words. It was kind of pathetic. I said, what's the point of getting all this money if you're so scared of it?'

'Was your relationship strictly platonic?'

'Wow. A voyeur. I've got some dirty pictures if you want to see them.'

I sat there, silent.

'Yes, we slept together. He got drunk one night and told me that he'd only had sex three times in his life before me. At his age. Wow. But I brought him along. I taught him a lot of things. And he taught me things, too. He was real smart, unlike the dweebs I usually sleep with. And he was real sweet. Until lately. He was really bummed about something. Maybe about the money or something. He didn't even cheer up when I bought him that Captain America jacket two weeks ago.' She wasn't the type to sob but tears silvered her eyes now and her voice shook. 'And I come up here and you tell me he's dead.'

'I'm sorry I had to tell you.'

'Yeah, I know, everybody's always sorry about everything.' She wiped her tears with her knuckles. 'But sorry isn't gonna bring him back.'

'So he never mentioned any enemies or anything like that?'

That wild laugh again. Unnerving in this situation. Maybe any situation. It hinted at the same kind of estrangement I was sure Jim Waters had lived with. There was nothing merry about the laugh. It was pure pain.

'Jimmy have enemies? Twenty-seven-year-olds with Captain America posters on their walls don't have enemies unless they're into video games.'

'Good point.'

She must have appreciated my smile because she smiled right back. 'Actually, I'm the video gamer. Jimmy didn't like them. He said they stressed him out. He was always talking about finding a place where he could be real peaceful. That's part of what our book was going to be about. This warrior roaming this planet looking for a place where he could lay down his arms. And just be kind of gentle the rest of his life.'

I stood up and punched in the number of headquarters. Kathy answered. 'Is the man there yet?' She said no. 'Tell him I'd like to see him tonight. Tell him where my room is.' She told me this sounded like an order. 'It probably is.'

Jenny smiled; a kid smile. 'That was pretty cool. It was like code. I don't have any idea who you were talking to. Or what you were talking about. You must be a superspy.'

'Something like that. C'mon, we need to get out of here. Unless you want to talk to the police.'

She was up from her seat and slinging her purse over her shoulder. 'Have you told me everything?'

She was bold, even brazen, but she wasn't particularly good at making her eyes say what her voice said. 'Sure.'

'I don't believe you.'

'Tough.'

'I need your cell phone number.'

'Why?'

'Because I may need to get hold of you.'

Her sigh would have made Hamlet envious. But she went over to the table with the printer and scratched out a number on a sheet of paper. She tore it in half and folded it over and then brought it back to me. 'I know I'm going to regret this.'

I took her arm and led her out of the apartment. 'Maybe you'll change your mind about telling me everything you know.'

'Haven't you ever given your solemn word to somebody? That's what Jimmy made me give him. My solemn word that I'd never tell anybody under any circumstances.'

We were walking toward the rear of the hall where there was presumably a back way out. We kept our voices low. The blare of different types of music covered us.

'We'll never find out who killed him unless we know everything.'

'I'll just have to think about it.'

When we reached the door I held it open for her. She led the descent. We didn't talk as we worked our way to the ground floor.

The night, all brace and filled with the promise of noisy neon life, was waiting for us and all of a sudden I wanted to be with a woman and a few drinks and having some laughs. This one was not only way too young, she was like working a Rubik's Cube.

'I need to go get stoned and listen to some of the CDs he liked.'

'Just keep thinking about helping me find out who killed him.'

'Man, you never give up, do you?'

'Not when it's important.'

'You and my dad would get along. He just harangues you until you give in. Only I don't give in.'

I had no trouble believing that.

Then she was walking away.

'I'll talk to you soon,' I called.

She gave me one of her typical replies over her shoulder. 'Maybe and maybe not.'

The only cash I had was a twenty so the bellhop who brought me my very late dinner got lucky. As I ate I went through the thirty-seven e-mails I'd received since the last time I'd checked. I was getting updates on all four of our races. Good news on two, fair news on another. Right now I had to put Jeff Ward in an 'Unknown' column. The murder could sink us. Even if we proved that Jim Waters' death had absolutely nothing to do with the campaign, we'd be smudged by it. Burkhart, like most of his fellow haters, made sanctimony one of his weapons. He'd wonder aloud if homicide wasn't something a ladies' man like Ward had brought on himself.

I caught the ten o'clock local news. On camera the scene at headquarters resembled one of those factory explosion shots. Real turmoil; mass tragedy. Since the reporters had little to go on as yet they took turns speculating on how this 'bloody death that police are hinting is a murder' would affect the Ward campaign. The footage they showed was of the dashing young congressman in his nightclub duds, of course. His trophy wife was the latest model.

When the news finished I switched to the radio. There were six local stations, only two with news staffs. They covered the story at much greater length than their TV counterparts but they made it even more suggestive and lurid. One even claimed that an officer who didn't wish to be named said that 'maybe a drug deal was involved.' The easy blame would fall on Burkhart; he'd somehow mind-manipulated all these reporters to trash Ward.

But no, this was just the American press we have today. And the blame isn't all theirs. We've been tabloidized as a culture. Left and right, both. We want news that sizzles and if it's not news, who cares as long as it sizzles anyway.

I was just about to open a few of the new e-mails when the knock came. The Glock I carried lay on the bed where I'd parked it earlier. Opening a hotel room door this late at night can be dangerous. You never get a fetching, willing woman; you almost always get a rumpled surly male with bad news.

Well, nobody would ever accuse Jeff Ward of being rumpled, but standing there in his bomber jacket and looking like a print ad for some macho aftershave, he said: 'I don't appreciate being summoned, Conrad.'

Off to a good start.

I opened the door wide and he came in as if he was in a hurry. He walked straight to the refrigerator where he helped himself to a beer. 'You know I didn't want you here in the first place. And now you're giving me orders?'

He had to take his anxiety about Waters' murder out on someone. I'm sure he'd unloaded at least some of it on his minions earlier but I was to get whatever was left of it. That is, if I'd allow it.

'That makes us even. I didn't want to come here, either, because everybody told me what an asshole you are. I only did it because your father asked me to. He called in the old times with my own father. That didn't leave me much choice.'

I thought maybe he'd see the humor or at least the irony in our positions but that had been expecting too much. 'Don't do me any favors, Conrad. You're just one more consultant and the same people who told you I'm an asshole probably told you that I go through consultants two or three a campaign.'

I sat at the table and watched him pace. I'd never realized it before but he had the looks of one of those old B-movie stars in the Saturday afternoon serials. The sleek, dark hair, the jutting jaw, the patrician nose. Hell, he already had the bomber jacket for it.

'This is all I fucking needed,' he said. He was talking to himself. 'Burkhart's going to be all over this. We were just catching up with him, too. I can't believe this.'

'I take it the police interviewed you?'

'What the hell's that supposed to mean?'

This guy was in pure paranoid mode.

'I meant what I asked. Did the police interview you?'

'Of course they interviewed me. So what?'

'So did they tell you anything about his death?'

'Do the cops ever tell anybody anything?'

'This is a waste of time. Get the hell out of here. I'll be leaving in the morning.'

'Yeah. And let me be the first to thank you for all the fucking help.'

'One of us is about to get his face punched in and I'm betting it's going to be you.'

'Oh, great, now you're threatening me. Dad can sure pick 'em.'

He was thirty-six going on fifteen.

'Why don't you sit down at the table here and shut up for a few minutes.' I'm not sure if he was afraid of me. I think it had all caught up with him. The anger in the dark eyes gave way to weariness. A great sigh as he tossed himself into a chair.

'You have a lot of faith in Nolan. You're going to have to sit down and figure out how you're going to handle a press conference.'

'Are you crazy? A press conference? They'd eat me alive.'

I wanted to say be sure you don't whine like this at your press conference but I'd probably ragged him enough already.

'It's too late to get ahead of the story. All you can do is try to stop the bleeding. Find the closest of Waters' relatives you can. Fly them here first class if you need to. Have them standing next to you at the press conference. Limit your opening statement to your feelings about Jim. Tell a few stories about how close you were. Make them up if you have to. Make everything about Jim. Then offer a ten-thousand-dollar reward for any information leading to the arrest of his killer.'

'Ten grand? Ten grand's not shit these days.'

'All right. Twenty-five grand.'

He shrugged.

'Then let the relative speak. Tell him or her what to say beforehand. Hopefully this'll be a woman and hopefully she'll cry a little bit. If it's a woman, put your arm around her when she starts to choke up. What we're trying to do here is set the tone for the questions. They'll still come at you but they'll look like insensitive assholes for doing it. A good share of the public hates the press. They'll be on your side to some degree. Especially if we get a woman and especially if she looks maternal in any way. You know that she really cared for Waters and just can't get over what happened to him.'

'And this'll work magic, I suppose?'

'No. But it'll make Burkhart's smear job more difficult to pull off. We've made the whole thing about Waters. The press'll be wanting to find some connection between Waters and his killer. Drugs or something. Or that he was gay or an addict of some kind.' I thought about his Captain America poster. I suppose that was a kind of addiction but one he well deserved. He'd been a lonely man. 'If you can find any kind of charity or cause that Waters worked for be sure to mention that, too. Soup kitchen, walks for cancer, that kind of thing. Start putting out press releases on anything good you can come up with. And be sure to mention a few of them at your press conference.'

'He worked at this soup kitchen, I guess. He liked this old nun. He brought her around one day to meet everybody.'

'That nun should be at your press conference. One side of you the relative, the other side the nun.'

'I'm glad you're not cynical, Conrad.'

'That's what I'm paid for. Being cynical. Burkhart's a bad guy with a lot of dangerous ideas. He has millions of dollars behind him already from the far right and lobbyists ready to give him a lot more if he wins. I want to stop him. You do what you need to. And you've run some pretty rough campaigns yourself.'

He helped himself to another beer. Walked over to the TV set and turned up the volume. 'I guess it's too late for any more news tonight.'

'Shouldn't your man Nolan be up here helping us figure this thing out?'

For the first time the natural arrogance of the B-movie face fell into uncertainty. I wondered if something had happened between Nolan and him. They were a famous duo in certain political circles. Where the hell was he?

'You know, I almost started laughing when you came up with that nun thing,' he said. 'This sounds like a *Saturday Night Live* skit. The grieving relative and the nun.'

'Desperate times. Now why isn't Nolan up here?'

'Family matters. He needed to be home.'

I doubted that. Nolan was a political junkie. A murder in the parking lot of campaign headquarters and he goes home after the police interview him? 'What's so important at home?'

'How the hell do I know? And what's so important about Nolan? You believe all that bullshit about him being the "brains" of my campaign? I don't need Nolan. He could quit tomorrow and I'd be fine.'

'Yeah? That's all you'd need. Your number one man quitting after a murder.'

'I didn't *say* he'd quit. I just meant that nobody's irreplaceable. What the hell're you trying to do to me anyway? You don't think I've got a million fucking things on my mind?'

There was something he wasn't telling me. Even the mention of Nolan had agitated him more than Waters' death seemed to.

'So what's going on with you and Nolan?' I said quietly.

He started to get angry, then thought better of it. He walked back to the table and sat down. 'Nobody knows anything about this. And I mean my old man. You tell him and you'll be sorry. I promise you.'

'Cut the threats. Just tell me what's going on.'

'Well, his wife and I—'

'Oh, shit.'

'You didn't even let me finish, God damn it.'

'You don't have to finish. Let me open my laptop here. I can write it out for you. Save you some time. I may not get all the addresses where you two shacked up but I bet I can get everything else right. I'll bet she's got a nice ass, right?'

'Very funny.'

'He's your best friend since grade school and you're schtupping his wife? Very nice.'

'Things happen to people.'

'Things like this don't happen unless the two people involved *want* them to happen.'

'She's always had her eye on me. Even back in college.'

'Oh, I forgot. You're irresistible. Also you can't help yourself when women throw themselves at you. Even your best friend's wife.'

'Don't get sanctimonious on me, Conrad.'

'I'm not. I'm being cynical again. I like your father. When I think of my dad I think of your dad. I want to make your dad happy by seeing that you win. So I'm thinking what happens if Nolan decides to go to the press? You're toast. Not only do we have a murder to deal with, now we have an affair. You know how many people will hate you for betraying your best friend and the guy who helped you win two terms in Congress? You'll be finished, asshole. Burkhart won't have to say a word. Nobody will. Because you'll have done it to yourself.'

I went over and got my own beer from the fridge. The cold air felt good on my face. Cleansing. I was in no position to judge him morally. I was in a perfect position to judge him professionally.

When I was seated again, I said, 'So where do you stand with Nolan?'

'He isn't speaking to me.'

'Since when?'

'Since two days ago. He won't answer my calls and when I see him he just walks away. He knows I won't start a scene in front of the others. I can't afford to. He might say something.'

'I'll talk to him.'

'He doesn't give a shit about you. Nobody here does. They resent my old man for forcing you on us.'

'You want to talk to him, then?'

The frown was petulant. 'I've already told you he won't talk to me.'

'Then I'll talk to him. By the way, when did he first figure this out?'

'Five days ago. Bryn was typing a letter to me on her laptop upstairs when one of their daughters hurt herself on the driveway. Bryn ran down to help her and forgot all about the laptop. David came home and saw it and read it. I'd written her this really sexy e-mail about us making love and she was responding. I was stupid even to send it.'

'Brilliant.'

'Well, fuck you.'

'You want me to tell you congratulations?'

'People make mistakes.'

He was hopeless.

'Have you talked to Nolan about it?'

'The one time I was able to talk to him I tried to tell him that I don't really give a shit about her. That it was just a little fling. Hell, he's had little flings. But he wants to make this big deal out of it. You know, make himself a martyr.'

'I doubt any of his flings were with his friends' wives. There's a difference.'

'Bless me, Father, for I have sinned.'

He was a peach all right. A real fucking peach.

'So we've got the murder and now we've got Nolan.'

He stared at his bottle of beer and then started peeling the label off with his thumbnail. 'Well, since we're playing Come to Jesus, Conrad, I guess I should tell you about one other thing.'

The headache cut down like a sword through the exact middle of my skull. What the hell was he going to tell me now?

'I,' he said, 'am being blackmailed.'

PART TWO

SIX

That night I had a highly erotic dream of a silver car and a license plate number. I was following the sleek machine on a narrow asphalt road through a dense forest in dangerous rain. I would speed up to eighty, once even to ninety, but I could never get close enough to catch her. The dream became a sweaty nightmare when my car plunged off a cliff, accompanied, all the way down, by the almost melodious sound of a woman laughing with great perfumed pleasure.

In the morning, my clock displaying 6:47, I called Kathy's number. She was yawning but awake.

'I apologize for this, Kathy.'

'Sure you do. I can hear it in your voice.'

I smiled. 'Actually, I do. Unfortunately, I need some help and that kind of takes precedence over everything else right now.'

'You're not even close to the record. At one of the places I worked, the boss would call me at six to tell me he was picking me up for breakfast at six fifteen.' Another yawn. 'So what's going on?'

'Do you have any contact with the local police?'

'There's a detective I used to date when I'd come back here from Washington. It was never a big thing but he was always a lot of fun. I've asked him for a few favors from time to time.'

'Good. I need a license number registration checked as soon as possible.'

I could tell she was smiling now, too. 'Can I at least wait until eight thirty when he gets in?'

'Hell, no. Call him right now. Even if he's in the shower.'

A sweet, girly laugh. 'Probably not a good idea. He got married six months ago. I doubt his wife would appreciate a call from one of his old lovers, especially before seven in the morning. So what's the license number?'

After putting some coffee on, I picked up my cell phone and started going through the messages I hadn't responded to yesterday.

The first one was the one I wanted least. Better to get it over with. I jabbed the right numbers.

Helen Ward answered. 'He's been waiting to hear from you. Can you believe all this? Just a minute.'

I hadn't said hello and neither had she. The old-time consultants had wives who acted like the wives of senators and congressmen. They were just as ready for battle as their spouses. She hadn't been unfriendly just now but all that mattered to her was that her son's campaign was in serious trouble. No other subject was allowed to enter her conscious mind.

Tom came on. 'I didn't sleep for shit last night. We got the news just before midnight.'

'Join the club. Jeff didn't leave my hotel room until two o'clock.'

'He's ducking me, the little prick. He doesn't want any advice from the old man.'

'I don't have anything new to report, Tom. But I told you I'd check in.'

'Helen's climbing the walls.'

'I don't blame her.'

'Where's David Nolan in all this? He's handled things for Jeff all their lives. I hate to say this but I trust his judgment more than I do my own son's.'

So he didn't know about Jeff and David's wife. He was seventy-four years old. He was overweight and drank a lot. He also kept the tobacco industry rich. He still smoked those small Chesterfields that had killed Bogie among many other millions. He'd had a stroke a few years ago. He knew about the murder. But he didn't know about the adultery. Or the blackmail. I wondered how much was too much to put on a man like him.

'Yeah. I got to talk to him. Real steady as she goes. Jeff's lucky to have him.'

'Just a sec.' He cupped the phone. I heard an angry voice. Helen. When he came back on, he said, 'Helen heard me say that about trusting David's judgment more than Jeff's. I thought she was upstairs. It always pisses her off when I say that. She says I'm being disloyal. To me I'm just being realistic. Our boy has a lot of good qualities.'

At the moment I couldn't think of any but theoretically I suppose he did. I mean if I really thought hard about it I could probably think of a few. Maybe.

'Burkhart's probably been jacking off all night,' Tom said.

'I'd imagine so.'

'You see those photos of him at the Creationist Museum? Little kids riding that animatronic dinosaur. The Europeans have always regarded us as hillbillies and by God maybe they're right. Riding dinosaurs, for God's sake. You think they really believe that shit happened?'

'Oh, yeah.'

'I don't know what the hell's going to happen to this country.'

'It's already happened, Tom. That's the hell of it.'

SEVEN

Yellow crime scene tape was the brightest color of the gray and cold fall day. Rain had turned the once colorful leaves sullen. A squad car sat next to the back door. The downstairs was a symphony of whispers. Mrs Rosenberg waved to me. It was obvious she'd been crying.

I climbed to the second floor. Apparently the no-smoking law was no longer being honored. I saw a couple of junior staffers hurrying toward me, both of them bearing cigarettes. They nodded and hustled on by.

David Nolan's office was empty. I stood in it for a few minutes and cursed Jeff Ward. There are moral politicians and immoral politicians. You'll find both on both sides of the aisle. You'll also find the sociopaths on both sides. Power attracts them. They feel it's their due. The hell of it is some of them vote your way, so if you want to keep the country safe from being overrun by the robber barons and the madmen you have to reluctantly support them.

I suppose Nolan had felt that way about Jeff Ward. He'd known him so many years he had to see what kind of a man Ward was. He had to have excused a lot in the name of friendship. Or maybe he drank a little of the heady wine himself. Washington is a gaudy young whore. She can make you feel important and in some respects immortal. You want to keep going back and back. It's the only place where you can get the magic wine. But then your ticket in, who has been your lifelong best friend, sleeps with your wife and you're forced to look not just at him but at yourself as well. How could you not see this coming with a man like Jeff Ward? You'd covered for him so many times with the wives of other men, why would it be any different with you?

Kathy Tomlin came in wearing a crimson sweater, black pencil skirt, and black heels. 'David was supposed to be at an advisory board meeting this morning but he didn't show up. That's really not like him. I'm worried about him. He's just such a decent guy. He really is.' She came closer to whisper. Her perfume made me fall in love with her. So did the finely-made face. A true pleasure to contemplate. 'Unlike another guy I could mention, I mean. David told me about Jeff and his wife. He is such a bastard. How could he do that to poor David?'

I wanted her to keep whispering to me but she had the nerve to lean against the door frame. 'If that ever gets out—'

'You think David might ever—'

She shook her head. 'No way. Even if he hates the messenger, he believes in the message. Burkhart is a fascist and I know we're not supposed to use that word because he isn't *technically* a fascist but that's what he is to me. I just wish we could get something big on him.'

I said, 'This campaign is so dysfunctional I don't know how you won two elections.'

'David Nolan. That's how we won two elections.'

Lucy came into the room looking as if she had absorbed the shock of Waters' death and was forcing herself to come back to the world of the living. She had even tricked up a nervous smile for us.

'Am I interrupting?'

'No,' I said. 'We're just trying to plan the day. How's the press conference coming along?'

'Pretty well. I've got both the nun and the relative. A little old lady whose voice trembles when she speaks.'

Kathy caught the moment. Grinned. 'Shameless, Dev.'

'That's what they pay me for. And even if we pull it off that won't stop the questions. Did Waters take drugs? Was he gay? Did he belong to a terrorist organization? The local hate radio boys and girls will be slandering him every time they're on mike. And they'll use that slander to paint our whole campaign.'

'He wasn't gay and he didn't take drugs and he sure wasn't in favor of terrorism,' Lucy said. As she spoke her voice rose defensively.

'God,' Kathy said, 'those brochures with Jeff in all those tuxedos and dinner jackets and with all those bimbos. Think what the radio jerks can do with them.'

'He told me they were all from very good families,' Lucy said. She sounded serious.

Kathy joyously put a maternal hand on Lucy's shoulder.

'Sweetheart, we know he got a bj from one of those very good family girls in the parking lot of a Burger King one night. And I mean outside the car.'

'God,' Lucy said. 'I forgot.'

Kathy smiled devilishly at me. 'That was probably the one and only time he was ever at a Burger King, by the way.'

I spent the next hour and a half going through every newspaper in the state. They all had extensive websites. Then I went to the sites of the TV and major radio stations. The coverage ran predictably. The conservative sources had already turned Jim Waters' murder into a mystery with hints of the diabolical. 'Friends said that although they liked him, he was often strange and secretive. He had worked as a speechwriter for Congressman Ward for three years, even during the time that the congressman was under suspicion for seeing several women outside his marriage.' Nice way to work that in. If they'd had more time they would have worked Ward's history to include bedwetting, public nose picking and leading terrorist cells in singing anti-American rap songs.

The more moderate outlets, print and electronic alike, weren't as hostile but most made the point that with the election so close a murder was not exactly what the congressman needed. They all cited the noon press conference and predicted that it would be well attended. Then I saw a quote from a fat junkie who had a radio show. It was a long quote. I could only stomach a few sanctimonious lines of it. God and family values. I wondered what any of his three former wives would make of it.

As I was about wrapping things up I decided to check on Burkhart's site. Any kind of official comment would wait until after the press conference of course but Sylvia had gotten her first shot in already. 'I want to offer the Waters family our true condolences. I'm told he was a very bright young man and an extremely hard worker. This is why it is so important that our youth get off to the right start. They get caught up in all these liberal causes and they lose their way. You can't have a mission that includes drugs and sex and a belief that big government can solve everything and expect to stay sane. I've seen a lot of my friends destroyed by these things in my lifetime. I certainly hope this wasn't the case with poor James Waters.'

Well, she hadn't included horse fucking anywhere in her list of liberal sins so I guess that put us ahead of the game.

When my cell phone toned I was glad to see the name Sarah Conrad on the caller ID. My twenty-two-year-old daughter was a senior at Smith. She planned to work for my firm over the summer as she had the last two summers. Then she wasn't sure what she was going to do. Right now she had a live-in boyfriend, Robert, who was an intern at a local hospital.

'Hi, honey.'

'Hi, Dad.' But it wasn't the usual happy 'Hi, Dad.' This one was serious. 'You busy?'

'You all right?'

'Dad, Mom has third-stage breast cancer.' Now I could tell she'd been crying.

Norman Mailer once wrote that the most powerful word in the world was cancer. He knew what he was talking about. I had a dozen thoughts and no thoughts at all. I had to say something, but what? 'When did you find out?'

'About twenty minutes ago. Andy called me from the hospital. She's there having more tests. Since he's a doctor there he can get her through pretty fast. He said she should be home in two hours.'

Dr Andy Connelly was the man Erin had left me for. I was long past blaming her; the fact that I was gone sometimes for three weeks running hadn't exactly been conducive to a good marriage. She warned me about it the last four or five years we were together. Her resentment, her anger, her loneliness. She was raising Sarah alone, she said. She was tired of going to movies and concerts and dinners alone, she said. She wanted me back, she said. And then one day she didn't. She came into our bedroom as I was packing and she told me about Andy and how she'd fallen in love with him and how she was sorry and how I could see Sarah just about when- ever I wanted. And how she had instructed her lawyer to ask for very little. Then she said she was sorry again and left the room. She wasn't waiting for me by the front door as usual with a hug and kiss. I have virtually no memory of the next thirty-six hours. Maybe an alien swooped down and picked me up and took me to the planet Evunom. Shock. I couldn't form coherent thoughts.

I was having the same trouble now.

'Andy said he'd like you to call her. She wants to talk to you.'

I didn't say it out loud but I thought how awkward he must have felt passing along that message. I'd met him three or four times over the years. We'd been painfully cordial with each other but when it came to real conversation we both floundered. I'd liked him more than I'd intended to. Sarah had convinced me over the years that he was a great stepfather and had made her mother very, very happy. Something I'd been too selfish to do, even though I'd always known that I'd never love anyone else the way I loved Erin.

'You'll have to give me her number, honey.'

'I've got it here. You ready?'

I wrote it down. 'Tell Robert I want him to take you out for a very good dinner tonight and get you drunk.'

Her laughter was frail but real. 'He's second shift at the hospital. That means if he does take me out it'll have to be after ten o'clock. The new head doc has it in for interns. He hasn't given Robert the day shift in three months. Only his pets get them.' Then: 'I'm scared, Dad. Robert's still here so he walked me through everything as well as he could without seeing a specific diagnosis. He told me how staging people can be deceptive. How it's not always as bad as it sounds.'

'You don't believe him?'

'He loves me, Dad. He loves Mom, too. He wants to make us feel better. I just hope he's not keeping anything back.' Then: 'Oh, there's somebody at the door. Can I call you a little bit later? I know none of us go to Mass anymore but say some prayers for Mom, will you?'

'I sure will, honey.'

> invasive
> non-invasive
> ductal carcinoma
> lobular
> phyllodes tumor
> angiosarcoma

These were just a few of the words I encountered over the next hour as I battled my way through at least twenty different websites dealing with breast cancer. An alien language, to be sure. One would give me a modicum of hope, the next would dash it. They were all dealing with the same facts, or so it seemed to my ignorant eye, so it was the writing that made the difference. I opted for the more reassuring assessments, though none were really all that hopeful anyway.

It was close to noon. I managed to get out of the building without anybody seeing me. I found a tavern six blocks away that offered the balm of beer and microwave pizza. You couldn't go wrong with that combination.

Kathy and Lucy were looking at a computer screen together when I walked past the conference room. Kathy glanced up and said, 'Dev, I've got some news for you.'

I walked in and helped myself to a cup of coffee while they finished up looking at some new demographic breakdowns on Ward's base. Apparently they were still worried that more than six percent of union voters would end up in Burkhart's column even though Burkhart was actively anti-union. The American tradition – voting against your own interests.

I sat at the conference table trying not to think about Erin. Work was my only hope. Work would keep me sane.

They finished in a few minutes.

Kathy got some coffee for herself and sat across the table from me. Lucy closed up the laptop and took it with her after waving goodbye to us.

'The Porsche was registered to a Pellucidar Corporation. I typed in the name on Google and got nothing. Then I tried Bing. No luck there, either. I found it ten minutes later. All that was listed was the name and the explanation that Pellucidar was in the business of selling audio equipment for stage shows and outdoor concerts. None of the names of the company's officers was familiar to me.'

'It could be a dummy corporation. You know, a cover for somebody who doesn't want to be known.'

'Burkhart?'

'Maybe. I'll call my home office. We've got an intern there from Northwestern who's really good at penetrating all these corporate names. Second year in law school and she's already a wizard.'

'Both CBS and NBC will be at the news conference. Their reporters have been spotted outside headquarters here.'

'Figures.'

'And our favorite not-news network is already asking, "What did Congressman Ward know and when did he know it?"'

'That doesn't make any sense. But it doesn't have to. All that matters is the implication. He's somehow involved in the murder according to them.'

She consulted her delicate wristwatch on her delicate wrist. 'I need to go help Lucy set everything up for the press conference. You've got my cell number if you need me.'

'Thanks, I appreciate it.'

'If David should happen to call in—'

'I'll see that you get to talk to him.'

I called my Chicago office. Howard Steinberg who runs the office when I'm gone got me up to date on all the good and bad news. The two main parties were about evenly balanced. No big surprises, either. We were still ahead where we planned to be ahead and still behind where we'd been from the start. But it was a tricky cycle this time and not even the best of polls could track the vagaries of public opinion very well.

I was forcing my way through some new internals, still deliberately not thinking about Erin, when my office phone buzzed. The receptionist downstairs said, 'There's a young woman calling for you, Mr Conrad. All she said was that her name is Jenny.'

'Oh, right. Put her through, please.'

When Jenny came on she said, 'Have you had lunch yet?'

'Actually, I have had lunch. Why?'

'I just wanted to talk to you. Could you stand just watching me eat?'

'As long as you use the right fork for the salad.'

'I know you think that's funny but my father is big on that stuff.'

'Not your mom?'

'She just does what my dad tells her. Makes life easier for her, I guess. The only time they disagree is about me. My dad would already have me on death row if my mom hadn't stopped him.'

'Is that what you want to talk about?'

'Now you're making fun of me again. I want to talk to you about what we were talking about last night except then I didn't want to talk about it.'

I smiled. 'I think I know what you mean.'

'The secret? Jimmy's secret?'

'Right. Jimmy's secret.'

'I guess I should break my word to him. I need to help you.'

'I'd appreciate that.'

'So you'll buy me lunch?'

'I'll buy you lunch if you can wait till one thirty. We've got an important press conference coming up.'

'Yeah. Man, they're really on Ward's ass. I've been watching the telly all morning.'

Telly. British. Cute.

'I cry every time they put Jimmy's picture on. I can't believe how much I miss him. I feel like I did when Roger died.'

'Who's Roger?'

'My border collie. And don't make fun of me. You live in my house, a dog's your only chance of staying sane.'

'I cried when my old tomcat Doc died.'

'How old were you?'

'Thirty-eight.'

'Are you shitting me? You cried about a cat when you were thirty-eight? Is that really true?'

'Really true.'

'Wow. Maybe you're not so bad after all.'

'One thirty then. Royale Hotel. The restaurant. How's that sound?'

'You and Jimmy would've gotten along. Especially after you told him you cried about a cat when you were thirty-eight.'

I actually did have a cat named Doc once. That part of the story was true. I sort of fudged the age, though. Doc died when I was eight.

EIGHT

While there are no punches thrown – at least not that often – press conferences are a form of boxing matches. There is a very real quest for a knockout. Under most circumstances Jeff Ward wasn't a household name outside his district. But with my least favorite not-news network already hinting that Ward was somehow implicated in the murder, the rest of the press, their tabloid credential intact, would be all too eager to follow suit. Maybe they would've been reluctant if he hadn't had the playboy image. But sex and now the death of one of his own staffers was too much to pass up.

Both sides here were performing a script. As far back as silent films you saw a mad-dog press attacking a pompous top-hatted politician on the steps of a government building. Reporters raging in silence for the head of the man they were stoning to death with their words. The pompous politician more pompous than ever. Until the fatal question. And then, in the way of silent films, a great melodramatic seizure of some kind when the question is asked. The pol clutching his heart; staggering, then falling. His aides grabbing him. A close-up of the pol's face as he dies. Jubilation on the faces of the reporters. All was right in America again.

TV has turned news conferences into gladiatorial contests. They're fun but sometimes I feel sorry for even the people I hate. I wouldn't do any better than they did.

All of us inside headquarters were tense. We stood at the front windows staring out at the press. I recognized the network reporters as well as the not-news reporter who was going to fry us for sure. Right now the camera people were shimmying and nudging into position for the best shots. The men and women vying for news stardom were checking their clothes and their makeup and their hair. The security people we hired were now in place around the narrow rostrum from which Ward would speak and take questions. The police were helping with the surging reporters. They doubtless enjoyed shoving the press around.

Everybody around me started applauding. Ward was downstairs now, talking with the staffers. He wore a very conservative blue suit, a white shirt that could blind you, and a tie more appropriate for a funeral than a press joust. On one side of him was Mrs Ruth Watkins. On the other was Sister Louise.

Mrs Watkins was smoking a cigarette and hacking. She was maybe five feet tall and around seventy-five years old. The baggy black dress made her appear shriveled. The voice said cigarettes and whiskey. In a crisis you go with what you can get. 'I don't know why the hell I can't smoke out there. I smoke everywhere else.'

Lucy was her handler. 'We won't be out there that long, Mrs Watkins. I promise you, you can smoke the second the press conference ends.'

'Well if it goes very long I'm just gonna light up.'

'The big thing,' Lucy said, her patience admirable, 'is to be sure about what we discussed. You told us you saw him many times growing up and you always liked him.'

Hacking, Mrs Watkins said, 'I *did* like him but I always felt sorry for him, too. He was such a weird kid. Everybody always made fun of him. Even my two kids. They did it real bad one day and I beat their asses, you can bet on that.'

'Remember we agreed to leave out the 'weird' part, Mrs Watkins. And I wouldn't mention beating your kids.'

Mrs Watkins had a hell of a good cackle in her. 'Honey, I'm old but I'm not an idiot. I know what you want me to do when we get out there. I'm supposed to put poor Jim in a good light. And I intend to. The poor kid loses his folks and then people pick on him all his life. Some life that was.'

Kathy was talking to the nun. Sister Louise appeared to be about as old as Mrs Watkins, a plump woman with a gentle face and a very gentle speaking voice. 'I just want to tell people about all the help Jim gave me at the soup kitchen. People always asked for him if they had a problem.' She hesitated. 'I won't say this on TV but I think this made Jim feel wanted and needed in a way he'd never been before. He was always smiling when he was at the center. Smiling and laughing. But when I'd have coffee with him somewhere else during the day – well, he never looked or sounded very happy.'

Now that he was coiffed and all shined up, Ward nodded to me.

'Well, how's all this looking to you? We've only got about five minutes before it starts.'

I didn't want to tell him that when Mrs Watkins first started talking I thought we might be in trouble. But now that I'd heard her out she was going to be fine, with or without her cigarette. Same for Sister Louise. 'They're the best kind of people to have with you. They're not lying or exaggerating. They're just saying what they believe.'

'Neither one of you is with the Mexican drug cartel, are you?' Ward joked.

The nun smiled. Mrs Watkins looked confused.

Ward had moved closer to Kathy. He spoke way too loud. 'I don't know why all this shit has to happen to me.'

Apparently Mrs Watkins, busy lighting up another smoke, hadn't heard him. I wondered what she would have done if she had.

When Ward turned back to the nun, Kathy made a face at me. I believe the word she was mouthing was 'asshole.'

I walked up front again. The reporters had replicated. Now our security people had joined the police in shoving everybody back away from the rostrum. Nobody seemed intimidated by the slicing wind or the scent of rain I smelled every time somebody opened the front door.

'The old man told me you're good at this,' Ward said, coming up next to me. 'I can be a bit of a jerk sometimes and I apologize for that. I appreciate you rounding up those two. They're good TV.'

'This still won't be easy.'

'I'm about ready to vomit and that's not an exaggeration. I don't know if the old man told you but my plan is to run for Senate after this next term – if I win. So this race is important to me for a lot of reasons.'

The sight of Ward in the window made some of the reporters go crazy, the way caged dogs would be if you were to run a steak along the metal links imprisoning them. In this case they wanted to vampire him.

'We about ready yet?' Mrs Watkins snapped somewhere behind me.

At least he saw the humor. 'Boy, she's one hell of a character, isn't she?'

'I kind of like her.'

His expression indicated that I was one strange guy. 'You trying to get into her knickers?'

But then Lucy was there. 'It's time.'

May God have mercy on our souls, I thought as we all shuffled toward the front door.

The press conference lasted forty-eight minutes. Mrs Watkins and Sister Louise were the early winners. They were good TV: Mrs Watkins' crackling voice that became more sentimental when she spoke at length about Jim Waters and Sister Louise's exuberance when she talked about all the people he helped at the shelter and how much they relied on him for their needs. You couldn't always predict how the media masters would edit an event but I didn't see how they could cut the relative and the nun completely.

Then came the questions for Ward. Most of us are actors. We know which face to put on at any given moment. And how to sound appropriate. This isn't necessarily insincere. If a person is weeping in front of you, you want to look suitably concerned. You put on the concerned mask.

I guess when you've been told all your life that you are one fabulous guy it's difficult to not sound fabulous even when you're trying to convey sadness. Ward gave it a good try – nobody had cared about Jim Waters more than he had; nobody knew as much about Jim's dream of an America that would someday live up to the aspirations of our forefathers – but it had a hollow quality. It was the wham-bam-thank-you-ma'am of goodbyes. I got a second opinion from the cold hard stare Kathy kept on him. She didn't seem to care for fabulous any more than I did.

The questions mostly ran to the obvious. Had the police ruled out a random robbery and murder? Had anybody around Waters noticed his mood being different in the past few days? Did Waters ever tell any of the other staffers that he was afraid of anything? The man from not-news was of course the first to storm the castle. 'Some people are saying (translated: my bosses who want a scandal are saying) that Waters might have known some secrets about your campaign that you were afraid might be made public.'

'So you're calling me a murderer? At least have the guts to use the word because that's what you're implying.'

'I didn't call you a murderer, sir.'

'You did by innuendo.'

'I just wondered if you wanted to refute all the whispers.'

'The whispers in your mind, you mean? From the big boss back in New York?'

'So you don't want to speak to that? Is that what you're saying?'

'I'm saying you're not a reporter. You're a flack for Burkhart. And that you've invented these so-called 'whispers' so you can help Burkhart in the election. Why don't you ask Sister Louise here or Mrs Watkins if they think I had anything to do with Jim's death?'

Mrs Watkins hobbled over to the rostrum and said, 'If my husband Norm was still alive he'd come down there and kick your ass for saying such a thing.'

Whoops of delight sounded loud and merry on this day of drizzle and chill. A media hero was born. An ass-kicking old lady who had put a hack reporter in his place.

Even Kathy was smiling. Our glances met. She looked snug and happy in the blue Burberry she wore.

In a single sentence Mrs Watkins had changed the shape and tenor of the press conference. Since there'd been little of news value in Ward's remarks the interest went to the old lady who provided good TV. As much as not-news was a disgrace to the profession, the other networks weren't in truth always much better. There's a great deal of sloppy, inaccurate, biased news available at the dinner hour every night across the board.

Ward knew how to play it. For the rest of the conference he kept his arm around Mrs Watkins' shoulder. Maybe he was trying to keep her from lighting up. That would spoil the TV image somewhat. Good grannies don't smoke.

Half the remaining questions were directed at her and she was ready for them. She was tart and crotchety and funny. And at the end sentimental one more time about her Jim. She had saved Jeff Ward's ass.

When it was all over, we went back inside where Joan Rosenberg was offering fresh, hot cookies and rolling a smart cart with two fresh pots of coffee on it.

I went over and shook Sister Louise's hand and then I went over – I had to wait in line – and gave Mrs Watkins a hug. I had to be careful not to get burned by the cigarette she had dangling from her lips.

NINE

J enny Conners was late, giving me plenty of time to catch up with
my other campaigns.

According to the internals we were starting to pull away slowly
in Madison, though we should already have been at least double
our lead by now. One race was still virtually tied and the fourth
one appeared to be coming our way. We'd made up four points in
the last few days thanks to an opponent who said that when he was
elected he would ban non-Christians from running for office and
would make homosexuality illegal. He said he was doing this on
direct orders from the Lord, who was apparently busier than hell
this election cycle. And it was clear by now that the Lord had no
more time for progressives than that not-news network did. Maybe
he was a stockholder.

So far my people in Chicago hadn't had much luck in identifying
the true owners of the Pellucidar Corporation. Its first address was
a PO Box outside of St Louis. Its present address was a PO Box
in Boca Raton, Florida. The man listed as the CEO didn't Google,
either. A mystery corporation and a mystery CEO. And a very
good-looking blonde driving a car that the corporation was paying
for.

I logged on to various local media outlets to see if anybody had
filed any stories about the press conference so far. Only one had.
The headline on that one was 'Gritty Granny at Congressman Ward's
Press Conference.' Under a photo of Mrs Watkins grinning, the line
was 'Wishes husband was still alive so he could kick reporter's
a**.' As I'd hoped, they didn't get to the murder of Jim Waters and
Ward's possible involvement until the third graph. What was more
important anyway? A homicide affecting a political campaign or a
gritty granny?

Essentially Ward got the kind of pass on the *Tribune* website that
would warm the black American Express card of any consultant.
They didn't lead with Granny but four graphs on there were three
different pics of her and a few colorful quotes she'd given out after

the press conference was officially over. Gritty grannies were a gold mine.

I could imagine Sylvia over at Burkhart's putting a cyanide capsule under her tongue. Though knowing Sylvia, she'd probably use a suppository.

I knew Jenny was here when the people at the table across from my booth raised their heads, quit talking, and began gaping at something approaching them. I was on the wrong side of the booth to see what they were ogling but I found out soon enough.

She looked pretty much the same as last night except now her black dress had silk sleeves down to just above her wrists. Despite trying to hide her attractive face and body in Goth she succeeded in being a beguiling figure anyway.

'Sorry I'm late. I went to church and said some prayers for Jimmy.' She didn't wait long to pounce. 'You look like you want to make one of your smart-ass remarks. If I go to church it's my business.'

'Glad to see you, too, Jenny.'

'My father says how can I be a Catholic and worship the devil? Hello. Goth people don't worship the devil. That's Satanists. Have you ever noticed that people who belong to country clubs are really dumb shits?'

'I take it your father belongs to a country club.'

'His home away from home, as he likes to say. My mother's there even more than he is. He says she's a booze hound; of course she says the same thing about him. I haven't seen either of them sober after seven at night since I was fourteen years old.'

'You're nineteen. You could always move out.'

She shrugged. 'I'm pretty spoiled. I mean, I could try to bullshit you but that's the truth. And my mother wants me to stay even if my dad does try to throw me out every once in a while.'

'Are you close to your mother?'

'Are you kidding? She likes to have me around so she can bitch at me. She's a real drama queen. When I was sixteen she found my birth control pills. She claims she had a slight stroke because of them and made my father call an ambulance. She was in the hospital for a week until her doctor said that there was a flu epidemic going on and they'd have to move her on a gurney to the parking lot if she didn't leave on her own. My father still tells that story. I always liked it, that picture of my mother on a gurney in the parking lot. You know, rain and snow and all that. She'd have a fifth of gin with her of course.'

She could wear you out with words. In self-defense I waved to the waitress.

I had coffee; she had the Caesar salad.

'Do you eat dead animals?' she asked.

'Sometimes I eat soy substitutes. Several people at my office in Chicago eat them all the time. I'm starting to get used to them.'

'I get sick to my stomach just thinking about eating a dead animal.'

'You mind if we talk about Jim Waters a little?'

'Oh, yeah, right. Well, first of all I should tell you that I really feel like shit about this. I gave my solemn word. Solemn. You know what that means?'

'I have a pretty good idea.'

She kind of threw herself back against the booth as if she'd been electrocuted. Then she crossed herself. I couldn't tell if she was kidding. She squeezed her eyes shut and said, 'Forgive me, Jimmy.'

The only thing I could do was wait through her sighs, her lower-lip biting and her nail drumming on the table between us. 'About a week before he died Jimmy told me that there was a kind of trapdoor in his kitchen. Only it wasn't really a trapdoor that led anywhere. They must have made it at the time the house was built. Anyway, it was about a foot deep and two feet wide, he told me. He said it was underneath the refrigerator. That's how he found it. One day he had to pull the refrigerator out because he accidentally broke a bottle of something and it was leaking everywhere. He didn't want it under the refrigerator. That's how he spotted it – the trapdoor, I mean. He said it was pretty cool. He wondered if it had been built when the mob was strong out here.

'Jimmy read up on the mob in this part of the state all the time. He thought they were pretty cool even though they killed people. Anyway, he said that if he ever wanted to hide something, that's where he'd put it.'

'You think he hid something there?'

'Maybe. It'd be worth a look.'

That one I had to think about. The police wouldn't have had any reason to move the refrigerator. The apartment wasn't the crime scene. On the other hand they were probably still going through his things, looking for anything that might lead them to the killer. Which meant that they wouldn't want anybody prowling around in there. And despite the fact that a trapdoor had a nice Hardy Boys ring to it, the chances of finding anything meaningful was a long shot at best.

'Your forehead wrinkles when you think.'

'Ah.'

'Makes you look older.'

'I see.'

'You're not a bad-looking guy from certain angles. But not when you're thinking like that.'

'I'll have to be careful not to think.'

'And to just hold your head at certain angles.'

'That, too.'

Halfway through her food, Jenny said, 'I can tell you're thinking again.'

'The wrinkles?'

'Uh-huh. Personally, if I had wrinkles like that I'd try Botox.'

'I was thinking of Botox for my butt.'

Her explosive laughter caused several tables full of people to gawk in our direction.

'God, I wish my father would say stuff like that.'

Every time she mentioned her father I thought of my shortcomings with my own daughter. She loved me and forgave me for all the times I wasn't there but I wondered if she had the kind of moments I did. I'd see a father strolling with his four-year-old little girl and I'd regret all the moments I could have shared with my own little girl.

'One of the things that's been giving me wrinkles is how we might get into Jim's apartment now. The police probably told the manager not to let anybody in. It'll be locked and there's probably a piece of yellow crime scene tape across it.'

'The manager? He's an idiot. I can get him to do anything. He thinks we're going to sleep together.'

'Why would he think that?'

'Because I sort of told him we would if he'd let me in when I forgot my key and stuff like that.'

'So you could convince him to let us in?'

'Not 'us.' No way he'd let you in. He'd get jealous if he thought there was something between you and me. You know, like you were moving in on his territory.'

'I see.' She was a passing fair judge of male psychology. We get territorial about women who wouldn't have anything to do with us even if we had a bag of cash and an Uzi.

'But when I get in there I can open the window off the fire escape and let you in.'

My recollection of the place – I'd only seen it at night – was that Waters' apartment had a fire escape running past his bedroom window. I also recalled, or thought I did, seeing the side of another apartment building next to it. I didn't particularly look forward to being seen on a fire escape in daylight.

I told her about that.

'Well, his wife works at the supermarket down the street during the day. He's always hinting that we could "have some fun" when she's gone. I'll just get Pierce to let me inside his apartment for a few minutes then you can sneak upstairs and hide somewhere.'

'I don't like the idea of you being alone with him.'

'He's a moron. I won't have any trouble with him at all.'

'What if he decides to stay with you in Jim's room?'

'I'll tell him to go get nice and spruced up and wait for me downstairs.'

At first I thought she'd had a seizure of some kind. Her body jerked and then jerked again. Her hands went to her Goth face and covered it. Her wail wasn't quite as loud as her laugh had been but now, when the other diners shot glances my way, they were filled with recrimination. Surely I'd said something terrible to this strange girl. Mean bastard.

'He's dead,' she managed to say. 'I just realized that I'll never be able to see him again. Never.' At least she kept her crying in the low decibels. 'I never thought of that till now. That I'll never be able to see him again. I loved him and his apartment and all his comic books. He was the only person who understood me.' Her mascara had started running. That much makeup, it wasn't a pretty sight.

'I'm sorry, Jenny.'

She plucked some Kleenex from her purse and went to work on her face. 'I know you are. And I know his other friends are, too. But sorry doesn't do much good, does it?'

'It's about all we've got.'

'I just want to go home and hide under the covers and pretend it didn't happen.'

'Can we go to his apartment first?'

'Oh, sure. I just need a little while to sit here and sort of suck it up. Is that okay?'

TEN

I don't know what she had to do but whatever it was it worked. When I peeked through the front door glass of Jim Waters' apartment building I saw that the mailbox area, which was on the right side of the vestibule, was clear. I eased in, surveyed the area, then began tiptoeing my way up the steps.

A few minutes after I reached the second floor I heard a door below me open and the oily voice of the manager say, 'Remember now, you promised.'

'If it wasn't my time of month we'd do it right now.'

'And I'm going to hold you to it, babe.'

Discreet he wasn't. He was broadcasting his infidelity to anybody who'd listen.

Two doors left, two doors right. One narrower door at the far left. I rushed over there. An interior rear staircase that apparently Jenny had either not known about or had forgotten.

I closed the door to the staircase and put my ear to it. Soon enough they made their way up the stairs.

'Hey, don't do that! You don't want to get caught, do you?'

'Right now, I don't care, babe. I'm just one of those guys that lives for danger.'

'Uh-huh. Well, don't I deserve a little respect?'

'I'll give you all the respect you can handle, babe.'

There would be so many pleasant ways to kill him. Shooting, stabbing, strangling, stomping, drowning, immolating. Or a combination of all of them.

'When did they put that up?' Jenny asked.

'Do not enter by order of the police? They did that last night. And it pissed me off, babe. Ruins the look of the whole hallway.'

So much for that spread in *Home Beautiful*.

'But remember, the cops hear about this, you got to help me out. You went up here by yourself. And you waited until you were sure that I was down to True Value or somewhere getting supplies. You remember?'

'I remember.'

'So what say I come in with you for a few minutes?'

Jenny was as surprised as I was. 'I thought you were worried about getting caught. What if the cops show up when you're in there with me?'

He had a sort of Cool Dude laugh. 'Like I said, I live for danger. It wouldn't take that long.'

I had to give him credit for that one anyway. Admitting he couldn't last very long.

'And I don't need none of those pills, either. I'm all man.'

'Please take your hand off my butt. Right now I'm thinking about Jimmy. He was my best friend.'

'No offense, but I never could see what you saw in that weirdo. But hey, takes all kinds, I guess.'

Now he was a philosopher. Definitely stomping and then setting him on fire. Make it real, real personal.

'All right. I'll stop and say goodbye before I leave.'

'I'll be waitin'.'

I heard her open the door. I was still waiting to hear him tromp down the stairs. All I could imagine is that he was still standing there, watching her. With his brainwaves on her butt.

Finally he started working his way back downstairs. But since I was dealing with a man who loves danger, I had to be careful. He might come bounding back up the stairs. I moved as quietly as possible. Jenny was in the door waving me in.

She closed the door behind me then put her fingers to her lips and her ear to the door. She was as suspicious of him as I was. We waited three minutes in silence.

She pointed to the kitchenette and the refrigerator. It was the same sort of Kelvinator my maternal grandparents had had. Meaning it was made long, long ago. The original color had been pastel blue but the harsh mistress time had faded it into a color I couldn't identify. That somebody had once stove in the bottom fourth of it with a few savage kicks hadn't helped the appearance either. Nor had the fact that the long chrome handle had been secured in place with a variety of tape over the years. The most recent was sturdy fiber tape. It seemed to be doing the job.

The fridge was wedged tight between a small stove on one side and the sink on the other. We wouldn't be able to wiggle it out.

We'd have to pull it out straight on. That wouldn't be easy. I remembered from last night that there wasn't much inside so emptying the contents wouldn't help.

'Sh-h-h.'

Then I heard them, too.

Footsteps. He was creeping up this time; an appropriate word. He was going to surprise her with greasy l-o-v-e. Valentine's Day had come early this year.

He knocked softly with a few knuckles. The apartment was tiny enough that we could hear him clearly even from here. I guess he was under the impression he was whispering.

'I got a little surprise for you, babe.'

She rolled her Goth eyes and gave him the finger. She strode to the door. 'I'm cramping real bad right now. Just please wait for me downstairs, okay?'

'Y'know, me'n the old lady do it sometimes when it's her time of the month.'

'Please just do what I say. Please.'

'I can barely control myself. You'll never forget it. I promise ya.'

Again she gave him the finger. What the hell, I gave him the finger, too.

Then the cavalry arrived in the form of a ringing phone downstairs. He must have left his door open because you could hear the ringing throughout the building.

'Shit. The owner of this pigsty said he'd call me.'

'Better answer it. Could be important. Maybe he wants to give you a raise.'

Or fire your ass, I thought unkindly.

'Yeah, shit.'

This time he took the stairs fast, swearing all the way.

'We'd better get moving,' I said.

I tried seizing the refrigerator by placing my hands on either side of it. It was heavier than it looked. The problem was that I couldn't angle it sideways even a few inches to help move it out of its slot. At best there was a half-inch on either side. Useless.

I assumed Pierce Rollins would be back soon.

Jenny came in. She'd been listening at the front door.

'I'm going to get in the sink and see if I can get enough leverage to push it out a ways. You go back to the door.'

I crawled up into the sink. Three inches separated the back of the refrigerator from the wall. I stood up and shoved my right arm to the center of the thrumming machine. I pushed. It moved maybe an inch. But it moved. I wondered why it would move with relative ease from this end but not from the other.

I hopped down and then got on my hands and knees so I could see underneath the front of the refrigerator. The big machine had been set on small wheels for easy moving. The trouble was that somebody had put small wooden blocks in front of the wheels at midpoint, I guessed as some kind of precaution. Nobody wanted a runaway refrigerator, the stuff of a sci-fi movie. So I reached back through a century of dust and grime and probably rat shit to dislodge the small encumbrances that had made my job so difficult.

I washed my hands in the sink before I went back to work.

No problem this time. I extracted the Kelvinator and left it standing in the center of the kitchenette. It nearly filled the place. I had to slide around it to find room enough to kneel down and search for the trapdoor.

And there it was. Ancient brittle linoleum covered the three-by-three outline of it. A small rusted handle sat in the center of it. It was like lifting a lid to check on a pot roast.

A rat toilet was what I found inside. The dried kernels of fecal matter formed an inch-thick bed on the wooden floor of the hidey-hole. And lying on top of this bed was a manila envelope that had been folded in half and wrapped tight with gray duct tape. I would have been more excited if the rat droppings hadn't suffused my senses and made me want to throw up.

I reached in and grabbed the package and crammed it into my suit coat pocket and then I did myself the favor of shutting the trapdoor again. This time I had no trouble getting the refrigerator back in place.

Then I heard the footsteps. The one and only Pierce was paying Jenny another love visit. The dear.

This time he'd brought his anger with him.

'You let me in right now, babe. I'm not stupid. I know somethin's goin' on in there.'

'I was just going to the bathroom, Pierce. God. I'm about done here anyway. I'll be out in a minute.'

'No. I wanna come in and get this thing over with. Ya know what I'm sayin'?'

She was frantic, gaping around as if she was lost and the roof was about to collapse on her in a second or two. There was only one way out and if we were seen, so be it.

I waved to her.

'Just a minute, Pierce. Just let me put my lipstick on.'

'No sense in that, babe. I'll be takin' it right off anyway.' I imagined he was winking to himself as he said that.

I pointed to the bedroom and she nodded.

Many of these older windows have been painted shut. Fortunately, this wasn't one of them. I got it about halfway up which was good enough. I helped Jenny through first and then I climbed through myself. I slid the window shut behind me and we began clanking our way down on a fire escape so old it swayed like an amusement ride.

When we were in the rental and driving away, I said, 'Pierce is going to be pissed.'

' "Pierce." ' I heard his wife call him Lou one night.'

'Figures.'

'You find anything?'

'Something. I don't know what it is yet.'

'Poor Jimmy. The last time I saw him, he was wearing that stupid Captain America jacket I bought him.' She sounded as if she couldn't decide whether to laugh or cry. She made a sound that was a mixture of both.

We drove back to the hotel in silence. She found a radio station that was apparently all rap all the time. I had my Glock in the glove compartment. I wanted to kill that station real, real good.

After I pulled into the hotel parking lot, I said, 'You've been a big help.'

'Will you let me know what you found?'

'I will.' But I didn't say when.

'By the way, I saw his aunt or whatever she was at the press conference. She's hilarious.'

'That seems to be the consensus.'

She started to slide out the door. 'My mother said that my father wrote Burkhart a thousand-dollar check last night and so did most of the people at the country club. I hope you can nail his ass. He's even creepier than Pierce.'

I smiled. 'You mean Lou?'

'Yeah,' she said and was gone.

As I was driving back to campaign headquarters I passed a billboard that came to me with the force of a religious revelation.

There she was in living black and white. Burkhart had his arm around her and it was only appropriate. The copy read: 'Help me and my wife take our country back.' BURKHART FOR CONGRESS.

It was the woman I'd seen snapping photos of Jim Waters.

ELEVEN

I got a cup of coffee at a Starbucks' drive-through and then sat in the parking lot taking the duct tape off the package with my pocket knife. Was this what Jim Waters had died for? Had he been given the chance to tell his killer where it was? Or had the killer simply meant to kill him and wasn't concerned with this small taped package? Then again – long shot – there was the possibility of a random killing.

I got it open. Inside the package was another package. This was wrapped in plain brown paper. But from the edges of the merchandise I had a pretty good guess what was waiting for me. One of two things.

The brown paper required only my fingers. I set it on the pile of duct tape and exterior paper. And there it was. I'd guessed a CD or a DVD. Turned out to be the latter. Nothing was written on the clear plastic container or on the DVD itself.

What had Waters gotten involved in? There are ops on both sides who break the law whenever they feel it's necessary. Had Waters been spying for one of them on the other side?

I started thinking about the dinner I'd planned to have with Waters. Had he been going to tell me something about spying or this DVD? For most amateurs involved in crime there comes a point where panic sets in. Second thoughts, doubts, terror. For the career criminal and the professional political op, the game has rewards that are both monetary and psychological. It's pretty cool pulling off stuff and getting away with it. A few years back an op from the other side had been charged in federal court for numerous violations of law. He was a past master at brochures that gave his clients deniability. They just magically appeared. Mostly they were sexual innuendo. He went in for quotes from people who claimed to have known the opponent at various times in his life. Both the quotes and the names were bullshit. But they kept the drumbeat of sleazy whispers going strong.

In a sleepy little town in Georgia he hired two white men gussied up in some kind of uniforms to misdirect the battered buses from a local black church. They told the drivers that there was a detour between the church and the polling places in town. They were directed to a dirt road that was laced with nails and broken glass and sharpened pieces of metal. The buses never made it to the polling places for the people to vote.

His greatest hit was phone jamming one of our candidate's lines for a day and a half so our man couldn't get his calls out. The election was decided by sixty-seven votes and the other side won. When the prosecutor started listing all the crimes the guy had committed the op couldn't help himself. He broke out in this grin that the jury could plainly see. He was proud of himself. The jury found him guilty on six counts and he was sentenced to eight-to-ten in a federal slammer.

I called my hotel on my cell. 'Is it possible to get a DVD player in my room?' I had an older Mac that couldn't play DVDs.

'Of course, sir.'

'I should be there within a half hour. I'd appreciate it if it was waiting for me.'

'No problem, sir.'

I spent ten minutes on the phone to the home office in Chicago.

'So you're not coming back tomorrow?' Howard, who runs the day-to-day far better than I ever could, said with a fair amount of exasperation in his voice. I prefer to be on the road.

'I know you owe Tom Ward a lot, Dev. But we really need to sit down with Finney and tell him to get his act together. He's desperate and it really shows. We need to help him.' Finney was a one-term congressman on our side who'd had, to be honest, a completely undistinguished first term. The word was he liked Washington night-life a lot more than he should have and the newspaper back home had started printing the gossip right from the start. Now he was floundering, damaging himself with pontifical speeches about the rights of all mankind and the greatness of America that lay just ahead, neither of which he gave a flying fuck about and neither did anybody else. The amazing thing was that he was only trailing a few points behind his opponent, another John Wayne-type who was always seen on the tube fondling his rifle with a suspiciously sexual pleasure. Finney could still pull it out but he didn't have much time. He'd dumped his previous consultant three months ago and signed

on with us. Unlike Jeff Ward, he hadn't accumulated enough gossip
to do him terminal damage.

'How about a Skype meeting?' I said.

'That'd be all right.'

'Go ahead and set something up and I'll be there.'

'That murder of yours is all over the fucking place.'

'Yeah, I know.'

'But I like that granny.'

'I've got an in with her. How about I line you up, Howard?'

He laughed. 'Actually, she is kinda cute.'

I was just about ready to leave the Starbucks' parking lot when
my cell toned again.

'Hi, Dev. It's Kathy. I'm glad I caught you. There's a detective
by the name of Fogarty who wants you to stop by the police station
as soon as you can. She said it's important.'

'But she didn't say why, of course.'

'Cops never say why. They have a badge. They don't have to.'

'Remind me to get one of those badges for myself.'

'Get me one, too, while you're at it.'

I'd never seen so much glass on a police station. The architect had
made it so friendly and accessible I almost thought I'd gone to the
wrong place. Kathy had given me simple directions but maybe I'd
misread them. But no, there above the wide glass double doors were
the words POLICE STATION. And on the sloping landscaped lawn
were hedges clipped with such fuss a king would have been pleased.

The interior was bright and open and the front desk was more
corporate than law enforcement. An attractive thirty-something
blonde in a short-sleeved blue uniform shirt was typing on her
computer. When she heard me she immobilized me with a white
smile straight from a toothpaste commercial.

I know men are supposed to have sexual fantasies every few
minutes or so but I divide mine between sex and romance. I'd had
a number of affairs since my divorce but none had led to anything
lasting. My fault, I'm sure. So when I see somebody as fetching as
this policewoman, sex and romance commingle in my mind and
romance often wins out. Yes, I'd like to go to bed with her but first
I'd like to get to know her. I gave up one-night stands after about
two years of them following the divorce.

'May I help you?'

And then she did it. She raised her left hand and upon a certain finger was enshrined a certain kind of ring, one generally associated with the institution called marriage.

'I'd like to see Detective Fogarty.'

'Your name, please.'

After I told her, she said, 'Why don't you take a seat over there. She's got somebody with her right now. But she shouldn't be long.'

This was the same speech you heard in dental offices.

I sat down on a tufted dark blue couch that was so comfortable I had to resist the impulse to close my eyes and take a nap. Detective Fogarty would no doubt be impressed if she had to wake me up.

She appeared in a few minutes, a slender black woman barely tall enough to pass the height requirement. In her white blouse and black skirt and somber black-framed glasses she resembled a grad student more than a detective. Of course there were clues as to her real profession: the badge and gun clipped to her belt. She didn't look much older than thirty.

'My office is right down the hall. If you'll follow me, please.'

She stood aside to let me walk in first. She pointed to a chair in front of her small metal desk. She was apparently a woman of few words. She closed the door then walked around to her own chair and sat down.

Numerous degrees, plaques, and a few photos of officials looking important covered the east wall. The right was given to framed photos of her family. All ages. A history there. If your eye was careful enough you noticed that the backdrop for many of the shots – including the two of her as a teenager – was the inner city.

She caught me looking. 'Vanity.'

'Not at all. The vanity is all those photos with you and those city officials. The family pictures are great.'

'You know I never thought of it that way. But you're right. That's a very good point.'

'I'm not as dumb as I look.'

She laughed. 'That remains to be seen.'

'Good one.'

She picked up a yellow Ticonderoga pencil and began to tap it against her left hand. 'I dragged you down here because you appear to be the last person James Waters talked to before he was murdered.'

'The last person you know of, you mean.'

'The last person we know of so far.' Then: 'I'm told you and he were going to meet for dinner.'

'He didn't show up.'

'Did he contact you to say he wouldn't be there?'

'No. The next time I heard his name mentioned was when I heard about his death.'

'That's when you met Lieutenant Neame, I suppose.'

'Right.'

'I'm taking over the case. The lieutenant is busy with two open cases that the mayor is very concerned about.'

'I see.'

She dropped the pencil in her pencil holder and then folded her hands on the desk. 'I realize that you didn't have much of a chance to talk to him. I've already figured out your itinerary for the day.'

'I probably spent seven or eight minutes talking to him in total.'

'But he still wanted to go out and have dinner.'

'Nothing notable about that, Detective Fogarty. Political people love to talk. War stories about old campaigns, kibitzing about how the new one is going. From what I've been able to gather he was a pretty lonely guy. Probably needed the company.'

She nodded and then gave me one of those assessing looks that are meant to intimidate. 'What if he knew something he wasn't supposed to?'

'If he did I don't know what it was.'

'But he wanted to go out to dinner. You'd met him in a meeting for a very little time and yet you invited him to dinner.'

'Well, "invited" is a little strong. We were going to have a little food, that's all. It wasn't anything formal.'

'Did you get the sense that he wanted to tell you something? Was there any urgency when he talked to you?'

In fact, there had been. 'No – I mean, I didn't notice any.' She wanted to keep me talking in case I'd accidentally say something she wanted to hear. I had to be careful. As much as I hated it, I needed to protect Ward, at least for now.

'I see. You weren't concerned when he didn't show up?'

'There was no chance to be concerned. Lucy Cummings called and woke me up from a nap and told me what had happened. That changed everything.'

'The staff people I interviewed this morning said that they were worried about James Waters. Said that he had seemed agitated lately.'

'Again, I knew him so briefly I had nothing to judge that against. He seemed anxious I suppose, but everybody gets that way when a campaign is this tight. And Burkhart has a lot more money than the Ward people do.'

'They're both wealthy.'

'True. But Burkhart has access to a lot of right-wing money. They're spending millions this election cycle.'

'That's what I hear.' She gave me the police stare again. 'So you're a hired gun.'

'In a way. I'm here as a favor to Jeff Ward's father. He saved my father's life back when they worked together. Tom Ward was my father's protégé.'

Her phone buzzed. She hit the intercom button. 'Yes?'

'Just wanted to remind you that you have the meeting in the chief's office in less than ten minutes.'

'Thanks, Julie.' Her full attention came back to me. 'So you're here just as a favor. You're an established hired gun who's seen all kinds of problems with campaigns over the years. I have the sense that you're also good at reading people. Picking up on their moods, maybe even their thoughts through their expressions and body language.'

'You're giving me way too much credit.'

She brushed aside my humble pie. Irritation crackled in her dark eyes. 'But somehow you don't pick up on somebody who to everybody else is clearly in some kind of distress. And he asks to talk to you and you don't sense any urgency.'

'I told you, you're giving me too much credit. I'm no mastermind.'

She stood up. 'If I didn't have a meeting I need to go to I'd keep you here until you started telling me the truth. I have pretty good instincts, Mr Conrad. To me it's obvious that there's something you're not telling me.'

'I don't like being called a liar.'

'Well, now you know how *I* feel. I don't like being lied *to*. And holding something back is a lie any way you look at it. If you want to get technical, you left campaign headquarters before our people could interview you – after you'd been ordered to stay.'

'Requested to stay. Not ordered.'

'You also lied to the apartment house manager about Mr Waters wanting you to pick up something in his apartment. You got there ahead of the police.'

'A good lawyer, and I have access to one, would be able to show that neither of those are violations of law. A) I've made myself available to you and other detectives and I've answered all your questions. And B) yes, I lied to the apartment manager but at that time there was no indication that Waters' apartment was part of a police investigation.'

'What were you looking for in Waters' apartment?'

'I'll be honest. I wanted to make sure his apartment wasn't some kind of drug den or sex den. Things the press could make something of. Very bad for our campaign.'

'How did you get in?'

'Somebody at headquarters loaned me a key.'

Bitter amusement in her intriguing eyes. She touched her sternum as if her stomach was sending up fiery spears of pain. 'No wonder people are cynical about politics with consultants like you running around. You're not cooperating one damn bit and you know it.'

She walked around the desk to the door. She opened it and stood back for me to pass through. 'I want a call before you leave town.'

Our gazes clashed.

As I started to walk through the door she said, 'And that's an order.'

TWELVE

I drove straight to the hotel.

The lobby was crowded. A banner read WELCOME PHARMA-CEUTICAL SALESPEOPLE! They were a prosperous-looking group standing outside the ballroom where their shindig was to start in a few minutes. I had nothing against any of them personally but their lobbyists were among the most treacherous in the business.

A prominent retired senator from our side now worked for their major lobbying firm. He didn't want to damage his rep as a progressive so he cheated. If you worked fewer than twenty hours a week lobbying, you didn't have to register as a lobbyist. He worked eighteen, nineteen hours and still got lots of great sentimental accolades on progressive websites. That's why I agreed with so much of the anger the anti-government people felt.

I poured myself a cup of coffee and sat in a chair in front of the TV screen. The DVD player the hotel had brought to my room was, thankfully, easy to operate.

The DVD had slid into the maw of the machine and was now posting electronic blotches on the screen. Then the show began. According to the counter, the DVD ran eleven minutes and twenty-eight seconds and then ended.

I watched it all, then clicked off the machine with the remote and just sat there thinking about what I'd seen and what it might have to do with the campaign and what it must have represented to Jim Waters. This DVD would have brought him money and the kind of vengeance he'd waited all his life to have. The outcast would have been the one in power now.

I made the assumption that he'd stolen it. He'd been a bright guy but collecting the kind of material on the DVD would have presented him with an insurmountable problem. Likely this was the work of an oppo researcher or private investigator. Millions and millions of dollars are spent every campaign cycle collecting damaging information on opponents. Both sides do it.

So we were back to stealing. Waters had somehow learned about it and somehow managed to steal it. And somebody took great angry exception to what he'd done. No doubt the object of confronting him had been to get the DVD back. But something had gone wrong. They'd killed Waters but had not gotten what they'd come for. Now I wondered what Waters had been going to do with it.

I took the disk from the machine and put it back in its clear cover. Funny how the presence of an object can change once you know its true nature. Before, it had been just another DVD in a world of a billion DVDs. Not even a barely-dressed twenty-something on a cover. Grubby, utilitarian. But after seeing it, it now had the presence of a highly classified document. The first thing I did with it was hide it in a suit jacket with a special liner. I never wore the jacket but I'd had it altered so that nobody could find its contents without ripping it apart. You'd have to pat the coat down to feel it.

I left the room and the jacket. I didn't want to haul the disk around. I didn't know who I was up against. And right now I wanted to go see the very comely Mrs Rusty Burkhart and ask her just why she had been following Jim Waters around. And taking his picture.

You could spot the Rusty Burkhart headquarters from several blocks away owing to the enormous American flag that had been set up on top of the two-story building. Given the weather, they'd probably been doing a lot of taking down and running back up lately.

The headquarters itself was emblazoned with red, white, and blue. Large color posters of Rusty Burkhart in various poses with his rifle covered the downstairs windows. Tinny speakers played a really annoying country-western version of 'Yankee Doodle Dandy.' You wouldn't think Burkhart would have much use for dandies, Yankee or otherwise.

Out front were three vendors: one giving away hot dogs, one giving away ice cream cones, and one giving away an assortment of soft drinks. Right now, even with the goodies being given away, foot traffic was thin and none of the pedestrians seemed interested. The silver Porsche was in a PRIVATE PARKING slot on the far side of the building.

When I walked in, a pretty teenaged girl in a red, white, and blue sweater rushed up to me and said, 'Just sign this pledge, please. We want to get a list of people who are real Americans.' Even her dark, curly locks were merry, bouncing away on her head.

I took the pledge card and read it. 'So unless I believe in every one of these points I'm not a real American.'

Merriment and enthusiasm died in her violet eyes. She really was a beauty. 'Well, I'd just say that if you don't believe in these points it's kind of funny you'd come here. If you're press you have to make an appointment first.'

'I'm not press.'

Confusion and anger spoiled her prettiness. She scorned me silently then said, 'Mrs Hawthorne, would you come over here, please?' Her voice had gone up a notch. She sounded desperate.

Mrs Hawthorne was a bulky woman of maybe fifty, dressed in an expensive and flattering gray tweed suit. She had her smile all ready for me by the time she reached us.

'Hello there,' she said to me. To the girl she said: 'How may I help you, Melanie?'

I wondered if she'd ever been a flight attendant. Her words had that syrupy, grating falsity.

Melanie nodded to me the way she would to a pile of dung. 'He doesn't want to sign our pledge card. The one about being an American.'

Mrs Hawthorne made the flight attendant schmooze even more syrupy. I could imagine what she was really thinking: *Everything's fine. You're embarrassing me and headquarters, Melanie. How many fucking times do I have to tell you NOT EVERYBODY HAS TO SIGN THE FUCKING CARD?*

What she said, of course, was, 'Melanie. Now we've talked about this,' smiling at me as she spoke. 'Signing the card is optional. Some people don't like to sign anything.'

'Anybody who won't sign this card isn't a real American. Mr Burkhart said that himself.'

Let me get my hands around your throat, you little bitch, Mrs Hawthorne had to be thinking. Her face was tight now and her eyes blazed. She was probably going to reassign the ardent Melanie to making sure that all the fax machines and printers had plenty of paper.

'Well, he didn't put it exactly like that, Melanie. I'll tell you what. Why don't you go and see if Phil needs any help with the mail?'

'I don't like Phil. He never pays attention when we stand for the national anthem.'

Mrs Hawthorne and I would never become fast friends but at the moment I felt sorry for her. Every campaign of either stripe has volunteers who can't be controlled. Windows get smashed at headquarters; door-to-door canvassing gets turned into arguments with citizens who made the mistake of opening the door; workers say stupid things in TV interviews. There are ops who encourage this. More of them on the other side by far but we have a few of our own. Mrs Hawthorne struck me as a pro at what she was doing. I admired her craft if not her candidate.

'I'll talk to Phil about that. Now why don't you go help him, all right?'

Melanie pointed to me. 'Be careful, Mrs Hawthorne. I think he's a reporter trying to sneak in here.' She stormed off.

'I'm sorry about all this, Mr—'

'Ketchum. Michael Ketchum.'

'I'm sorry about this, Mr Ketchum. Once in a while our volunteers get a little too enthusiastic. Melanie has a tendency to go overboard.' She raised a hand upon which had been bestowed a wedding ring that would easily pay for a year's tuition at an Ivy League college. She indicated with a sweep of her hand how busy and industrious everybody was. And they were. I counted seventeen people working the phones, reminding people of why they should vote Burkhart and making sure that they planned to vote. And offering rides if needed. This was the ground war and it had damned well better be good. This one looked all *too* good. 'Did you want some information on Mr Burkhart?' The flight attendant smile. She was heavyset but the pleasant face had kept its charm. 'Some people still haven't made up their minds. So they stop in to pick up brochures. They take them home and study them with their spouses. We believe that if you put us alongside our opponent we'll look very good. Mr Burkhart was never a playboy, thank goodness.'

The little dig. It's almost impossible to resist. You're in a war. You've convinced yourself that the person you're running against takes calls from Satan at least four times a week. The mere mention of his or her name unhinges you and your knife appears in your hand. This is all internal. In public you need to present yourself as rational and professional.

'I was wondering if I could speak with Mrs Burkhart.'

The narrowed eyes, the second-thought reassessment. She had to be thinking that maybe Melanie was correct after all. Maybe I was a reporter trying to sneak past the guards to try to humiliate Mrs Burkhart in an interview.

'Do you know Mrs Burkhart?'

'Not really. But she was taking some photographs and I wondered if I could get some copies of them.'

'Some photographs? I'm afraid I don't understand.'

She appeared in the rear of the factory-like room. Even from a distance she was as imperious as a Hollywood goddess.

'Mrs Burkhart!' I called and started moving fast up the center of the aisle.

'Please, Mr Ketchum. You shouldn't—'

But I was pounding up the aisle in long strides. Mrs Burkhart was paying no attention. She hadn't heard me call her name above the din.

When I reached her, she was just about to walk through the door she'd just come out of. 'Mrs Burkhart! Mrs Burkhart!'

She turned. She was a gorgeous, golden animal kept gorgeous by an army of men and women whose job was to help her defy age and fashion. Her face had the wisdom of carnality in it, that immortal knowingness of how to please and control men. Even the brown eyes, no doubt courtesy of contacts, had a golden glow to them. Those eyes assaulted you. Today she wore an emerald suit of silky material that swept the long, lean lines of her body with a true majesty. In addition to sexuality she also radiated strength and health. I wondered if she'd try to beat the shit out of me. I was sure she had it in her to try.

'Is there something I can do for you?' She had to be careful. I was a peon but maybe I was a connected peon and maybe my connection wouldn't appreciate her pissing on me. Of course she couldn't quite keep the disdain from her tone.

I got close to her and said, 'I saw you taking pictures of James Waters. I'd like to know why you were doing that.'

She touched her hand to her handsome bosom. Before she could speak, Mrs Hawthorne, breathless, arrived.

'I tried to stop him, Mrs Burkhart. But he got ahead of me.'

Mrs Burkhart's eyes scathed the well-fed body of her employee and said, 'I suppose you did your best, Mrs Hawthorne. You should get into that exercise class I keep telling you about. I go three times a week and I don't even need it.'

Mrs Hawthorne's eyes showed real pain. Humiliation, I guessed. This was the second time I'd been forced to feel sorry for her and I didn't even like her.

'So it's all right if he stays?' she said.

'I'm sure I can handle this, Mrs Hawthorne. Thank you so much for your usual help, though.'

Mrs Hawthorne, whipped, looked at me then lowered her head, turned around, and headed back to the front.

'Maybe slapping her would've been kinder than what you did.'

The golden eyes shimmered with royal anger. 'I don't know who you are but I already don't like you. We'll go outside to talk and don't say another word till we get there.'

She led the way to a side door and to the chill, gray day. Her perfume was so seductive I felt a need to touch that Cleopatra flesh of hers. Though her hair didn't look overly lacquered, the blonde perfection of the chignon was not ruffled by the wind.

'Who the hell are you?'

'Just somebody who saw you snapping Waters' picture.'

'And you knew Waters?'

'Slightly. Not very well.'

She managed to get a long cigarette going and took a deep diva-like drag on it. She dispersed it with those rich, erotic lips. 'All right, you saw me taking his picture. And that's supposed to mean what exactly?'

'That's what I'm curious about. Why you'd be taking photos of Waters, especially since somebody killed him later that night.'

If any of this was intimidating her, she managed to disguise it with her irritated glances and tone.

We listened to the red and gold and brown leaves skitter like forlorn little creatures across the asphalt of the parking lot. Finally I said, 'I haven't gone to the police. Not yet.'

'I want to see some ID.' The salon seductress suddenly sounded like a cop.

'If I show you, you'll know who I am.'

'Oh, right, I suppose you're somebody famous.'

'My name is Dev Conrad. I work for Jeff Ward.'

'You bastard!' Her cigarette went flying as she lunged for me, shoving me back into the rear of a parked car.

She wasn't as strong as I'd thought. 'I need to figure out if you were just doing some campaign dirty tricks or if you have something to do with Jim Waters' murder. Since you're unwilling to help me, maybe your husband can bring me up to date on all this.'

'Leave my husband alone. He's got enough problems.'

Odd thing for somebody to say. Her candidate had come from behind to lead us by three points. I wondered what she was talking about.

She smiled. She had lovely teeth and a deceitful smile. It said *aw, shucks* and I didn't believe any of it. 'You caught me.'

'I did?'

'I was taking photos of Waters because I was going to send one of our girls to 'accidentally' meet him in a bar and get him drunk and see if he'd tell her anything.'

'A spy operation.'

'Exactly.'

It was bullshit. Given her fantastic presence I resented her for not being better at the game. 'Pretty clever.'

'So you see it's no big deal. I hope that satisfies you.'

It didn't, but she was going to stick to her silly story no matter what I said. Detective Fogarty and I could agree on one thing anyway. Something was going on here and so far none of us had a clue except me. I had that DVD. I knew what I'd seen but so far the only clue I had to its meaning was Jeff Ward's admission that he was being blackmailed.

'That was the easy part, Mrs Burkhart.'

'What're you talking about?'

'You're lying and we both know it. I'm guessing you're involved in something pretty bad – and you're too scared to think straight.'

I have to admit that her scornful laugh sounded pretty damned confident. 'Do I look scared? Do I sound scared? The only reason I was leery of you when you started chasing me inside was because I didn't know who you were. There're a lot of freaks who hang around political campaigns. I thought you might be one of them.'

The triumph in her voice – the princess of the realm to the commoner – only increased when the side door opened and a woman called out, 'Mrs Burkhart. We need you inside.'

Her smirk was one of jubilation. 'I'll be right there.' Then: 'I need to go inside and I'd advise against trying to stop me. I'd hate to call the police and tell them that somebody from the Ward campaign was accosting me.'

'This isn't over.'

'I wouldn't bet on that. My husband is a very powerful man.'

The woman held the door open for her. Waiting.

'Tell her you need a few more minutes out here.'

'I will not.'

I slipped my cell phone from my jacket pocket. 'You don't have to call the police. I will. I'm going to take this cell phone and call Detective Fogarty at the police station. She'll be very interested when I mention that you were taking photos of Jim Waters the day he died. You'll have to do a lot better with your story than you did with me.'

She gritted her teeth. 'I'm so sick of threats.'

One more word to add to my Burkhart vocabulary. Problems, threats.

'I'm also sick of men. Men fuck up everything.'

Somehow I didn't think she was speaking in the feminist sense. She'd probably run up against a man or men who wouldn't let her have her narcissistic way. She was an expensive toy for men who could afford her.

'Are you going to tell me what's going on, Mrs Burkhart?'

'Just wait a minute.'

'For what? This is getting us nowhere.'

'I need some time.'

'That's up to you, Mrs Burkhart. I thought maybe I could help you out a little. That's why I stopped by. But I can see you don't want any help, do you?'

She had a harsh Gucci laugh. 'How can you say that with a straight face? My God – you stopped by to help me out a little. You stopped by because you want to get my husband in trouble.'

'If that's the way you choose to look at it, Mrs Burkhart, that's up to you. Now please get out of my way. I've got things to do.'

She clutched my sport coat. She wasn't restraining me as much as she was pleading with me. I doubted she played the supplicant very often.

'Give me until tonight before you do anything, including the police. I have to make some decisions. I'll give you my cell number. Then we can talk.'

She dug in her purse and extracted a business card. 'Turn around.'

This was the Mrs Burkhart I'd come to know and love. Barking orders. As she scribbled her cell number on the card she had pressed to my back she kept up a stream of whispered curses. I had the feeling they were aimed as much at herself as at me.

'There. You can turn around again.'

'Thank you, Your Highness.'

'You know, I really don't like you.'

I took the card. 'You wouldn't be surprised if I said the feeling is mutual, would you?'

But she was done with me. 'I expect you to keep your word.'

I hadn't given my word but she was so used to getting her way she just assumed I'd pledged undying loyalty to her throne.

By the time I'd backed out and started for the street, she was rushing through the side door and into the maelstrom of the campaign.

THIRTEEN

I bought a grilled cheese sandwich and a Caesar salad and a beer in the hotel café and took them up to my room. I worked while I ate. In addition to interviews the DVD held names of people and places. I needed to verify that these actually existed. In the age of photoshopping you had to check and recheck everything.

The first two names checked out. I found them in the white pages online.

I finished my food. I still had half my beer. I worked on the bottle as I punched in phone numbers. Three rings, four rings.

'Hello.' Female. Wary.

'Mrs Hayes?'

Silence.

'Mrs Hayes?'

'Who is this?'

'My name is Dev Conrad. You don't know me, but I'd like to set up an appointment to see you.'

Long pause. 'Those days are behind me. Now leave me alone.'

She slammed the phone with a fury that told me how much she wanted to forget her past and resented – despised – anybody who'd bring it up.

The second number I dialed yielded only an automatic message voice, one of those robots who will someday be our masters. The robot wouldn't even part with the name of who owned this particular phone number. I left no message.

I called Ward headquarters and asked for Lucy.

'I was getting worried about you. We hadn't heard anything from you. Jimmy's murder has really freaked me out. And I haven't said "freaked me out" since college.' I could feel her smile over the phone, a fresh, appealing young woman who just happened to be smart as hell.

'I'm fine. Just busy. I wanted to ask you about your newspaper contacts. Do you know anybody friendly on the *Winthrop Times*?'

'I do, as a matter of fact. Why?'

'I'm doing a background check on something. I just need to talk to somebody from the area who won't mind answering some questions.'

'This sounds mysterious.'

'Not really. I'm trying to check on some brochures that are circulating down there claiming that Jeff's family managed to get two DUI charges expunged from police records in Winthrop.'

'Wow. When did this come up?'

It came up as I spoke the words. Sometimes my facility with lies amused me; other times it depressed me. After a few too many drinks I liked to think of myself as a noble knight fighting an honorable war. After a certain amount of liquor you can rationalize any number of sins.

'Somebody in my home office picked it up from one of our ops and then they phoned me with it. But please don't share this with anybody on the staff, all right? No need to worry about it until I can verify it. So far nobody's actually seen one of these brochures.'

Urban legends prosper in campaigns on both sides. Did somebody accuse my opponent of being a horse-fucking, grave-robbing child murderer? Gosh, I just can't imagine how a story like that got started (after your minions had been whispering it for weeks).

'That's so ridiculous. If that was true we would have heard about it a long time ago.'

'We're in a tight race and running out of time. Anything goes now.'

'Oh, I met that Detective Fogarty. She was just here. She's pretty cool. She said she talked to you.'

I had to give Fogarty her relentlessness. This was the sort of case that would get a detective noticed in the press.

'Well, I'll be there in a while, Lucy. Now how about the name of that reporter in Winthrop?'

'Oh, sure.'

She told me. I entered name and phone and e-mail into my Mac laptop. 'I appreciate it, Lucy.'

Nan Talbot was in a meeting but was expected back in fifteen minutes or so. Would I like to call back then?

In twenty minutes I called again. I used Lucy's name more often than I probably needed to, but given the kind of questions I was about to ask she needed to trust me. And every time I used it, Nan Talbot said something flattering. 'She's one of the few political press people I like. Very straightforward. A lot of them are just flacks. They don't do anything but brag about their candidate and if you ask them anything serious about an issue they can't give you a coherent answer. Lucy can do it all – and talk and write and really walk you through any issue you have questions about.'

'Well, she said you might be able to help me.'

'I'll sure try but I have to warn you that I need to leave on a story in about fifteen minutes.'

'I keep thinking of the right way to bring this up—'

'Boy, this should be good—'

'I need to know about a house of ill repute you had in Winthrop about five years ago.'

She laughed. 'A popular subject. I'm from Des Moines. I've only been here for two years or so, but last winter a private investigator asked me pretty much the same thing and I had to go ask the people who'd been here a long time.'

'A private investigator?'

'Yes. He wanted the background on the house and where he might find Vanessa La Rouche. The first thing I told him was that was her – I don't know what you'd call it – stage name, I guess. Her real name was Sandy Bowers. She was the madam of the place. Then I had to tell him that I had no idea where she went after the state shut her down. She operated for four years here, two terms of the same mayor. He protected her. Some said she had something on him and some said it was a straight payoff. Whatever, when the mayor got voted out she didn't last long.'

'Has anybody ever heard from her?'

'Not that I know of.'

'How about that private investigator? Would you happen to remember his name?'

'No. But it's somewhere on my computer. I'll look it up when I get a chance. You have an e-mail address?'

I gave it to her.

'What happened to the girls?'

'That's what made her place so special. That's why she got so many important people going there. Winthrop's economy went down the tube in 2005. Three big manufacturing plants went under and so did a bank. The feds closed it. Sandy or Vanessa was smart. She used only housewives. You know what MILFs means?'

'Mothers I'd Like to Fuck?'

'Exactly. Really attractive, clean, bright women whose husbands were suddenly on unemployment insurance. Very discreet. Appointments only, because not all of them could work every night. Juggling the hours was the most difficult part, I assume. They had families. Hard to know if the husbands really knew or not. But she raked it in and the people here said that the housewives made good money, too.'

'Any scandals?'

'None that left that house. Of course, there were always rumors.'

'Such as?'

'Well, seems a certain well-known lawyer from Galesburg liked to argue about the kind of money he had to pay Vanessa, so he threatened to go to the local news media. I don't know who Vanessa called but she had an angel somewhere. Everybody figures it was the mob. They kneecapped the lawyer and then started sending him photographs of his kids just to remind him how vulnerable he was.'

'Doesn't sound like the kind of lawyer I'd hire. If he dumped on the house he'd be admitting he was not only a client but that the reason he was doing it was because he was too cheap to pay the going rate. He'd look pretty bad.'

'Well, if you knew the guy you'd understand. He's all bluster, very pompous and very loud. Really obnoxious.'

'But even that isn't much of a scandal. He didn't go to the press after all.'

'Vanessa or somebody knew what they were doing. As I said, everything stayed in the house. Hey – I need to go.'

'Thanks. And I appreciate you sending me that investigator's name.'

'It'll be a little later today. Say hello to Lucy for me. Tell her my boyfriend's got a guy she should meet. He thinks they'll really hit it off.'

'Will do.'

At least I was beginning to see the schematic. Somebody hires a private investigator. Private investigator gets video. Video becomes blackmail source.

But who hired the investigator? And where did Mrs Burkhart fit in?

FOURTEEN

It was time to call Erin. Every tenth thought had been of her since Sarah had called me. Third-stage cancer. Impossible. Her face at our wedding; her face in the hospital bed the night she delivered Sarah; her face watching Sarah in a third-grade play. Beautiful, smart, funny, sad Erin. So many things. And so many times now I wished she were still my wife.

I opened a beer, parked myself at the table and then spread flat in front of me the piece of paper I'd written Erin's number on. I placed it next to my cell phone.

I was trying to prepare myself. I wanted to sound friendly and concerned as soon as she answered. I wanted to let her know how much I still cared about her. I wanted to talk about Sarah, because after we discussed Erin's health that would be the subject that bound us together. Mother and father of our beautiful daughter.

I just didn't want to say the wrong thing. She was going through hell and I didn't want to make it worse for her in any way.

I swigged some beer and set the bottle down again. I took a deep breath, the way those kids in South America must do just before they dive off the sides of mountains into the sea.

Erin's voice had changed considerably. It said: 'This is Dr Connelly speaking.'

I'd assumed Sarah had given me Erin's cell phone number. Not the residential one.

For years I'd thought of him as the man who'd broken up my marriage. But after I started being honest with myself, I realized that our marriage had been over long before he came along.

'Hello? Is this Dev?' My name had come up on his caller ID.

'Yes. I'm calling to see how Erin's doing.'

'She's a strong woman, as you know. But naturally at a time like this she's thinking about her entire life. She wanted to talk to you. You're important to her, Dev. It'll help her just to hear your voice.'

'She's a good woman.'

There was a pause. 'Look, Dev, I know this is awkward for you.

It's awkward for me, too. But there's always been something I wanted to say to you. Erin tried but she thinks you don't believe her. A month and a half before I even met her she'd gone to her attorney and started proceedings. If that hadn't been the case I would never have asked her to have dinner with me. I hope you believe that.' Another pause. 'The main thing is that she needs us both right now.'

'I agree.'

'By the way, Andy is what my friends call me.'

'All right, Andy. Can she talk on the phone now?'

'I'll get her in a second, Dev. But there's one more thing I need to explain. She's going to ask you to fly out here to be with Sarah and me on the morning she has surgery. I want you to know that I'm all for that. When she's in post-op and wakes up with the three of us standing around her, that'll be a big boost for her, believe me.'

I wanted to hate him but he wouldn't let me. A part of me was still nursing The Wronged Husband; his concern was for the woman he loved. His ego didn't matter. She had invited her ex-husband to come to her bedside. He was that rarest of beings: a real adult. The sneaky bastard.

'You don't have to make your mind up now, Dev. But please give it serious thought.' In his laugh I heard fatigue. 'I'm sure Sarah'll be working on you about it. Now I'll get Erin.'

There was a minute's wait and then she came on the line, a voice from a shared past of memories that still had the power to crush, of a love I knew I'd never find again, a love that I had taken for granted and wasted.

Another phone clicked off as Erin said, 'Remember that spooky fortune teller we went to in New Orleans?'

We'd honeymooned there for a week. I was on a brief leave from the army. One night we'd been giddy on wine and each other and had stumbled along steamy summer streets into an area that seemed to have all the remnants of a deserted circus scattered along shadowy broken sidewalks. We'd gone to an elderly woman who smelled of onions and cooking oil and marijuana. Her crystal ball was cracked down the center. We'd both been laughing as we went in, as I imagined most of her customers did. But soon enough Erin was taking the woman very seriously.

This was the living room of a house that should have been

condemned forty years ago. It tilted when we entered it. The wood reeked of age, a vinegary odor. Black curtains divided the room in half. The woman and her attire were strictly central casting. Gypsy fashion cut for a woman of enormous size. The Day-Glo posters of astrological figures were diminished in impact thanks to her sad old dog that kept peeing on the floor about a foot from my leg. He licked his chops so loudly he almost drowned out his magical owner.

The woman – Madame Celestia, as I recall – went through the usual mumbo jumbo in a droning voice. I didn't pay much attention. I just wanted to get out of there. Erin was spellbound.

Then Madame Celestia's phone started ringing somewhere behind the curtained area in her tiny front room. She wore so many beads and chains she clacked and jangled as she moved. So much for show business. She hefted her considerable body from the chair, farting as she did so, and then plowed through the separation in the curtains only she could see. She left with no explanation or apology. Soon enough the phone stopped ringing and she was shouting at somebody in Creole. Whoever had called had made her mightily pissed.

After slamming the phone down, she reappeared. 'I must help someone the dark gods have captured. I am also a witch and know the magic to free him.'

Drug connection? Cops about to land on her?

Then, remembering that she hadn't concluded Erin's reading, she leaned forward with alien eyes and said, 'Oh, yes, before I forget. You will lead a charmed life.'

As she disappeared again, I started laughing, which irritated Erin. On the sidewalk she snapped, 'You heard what she said and you're laughing? I'm going to have a charmed life.' She was gorgeously silly and drunk.

But our argument was brief. Within twenty minutes we were walking along the river where we found a park perfect for making honeymoon love. How I had wanted that moment to freeze in time; there were nights after our divorce, and in my worst lonely drinking, when I would reach out to snatch the memory as if it were a golden bird.

'I want my money back from Madame Celestia. Do you remember her?'

'Vividly.'

'The whole "charmed life" thing?'

'I don't blame you. I think you should get a lawyer and sue her.'

I could hear giggling. 'God, this is the first time I've laughed in a few days. It feels great. Thanks.'

'I charge for stuff like this, you know.'

'Keep me laughing and I'll send you whatever you want.' Then: 'I'm sorry the way we ended up and how strange it all got, Dev. I didn't handle it very well. I was so angry with you, I didn't consider your feelings. I hadn't cheated on you but it felt like it – marrying Andy so quickly, I mean. You know how much I loved you for so long, Dev. And now that this has happened – I just wanted you to know that one of the most comforting things I have is my memories of us in the early years. You're still with me, day in and day out. I still hear you and sometimes I think I even see you, but it just turns out to be a stranger. I just wanted you to hear me say that.'

'I feel the same about you, Erin.'

I wanted to hold her, kiss her, make her better. And Dance Her to the End of Time, the song she'd played over and over.

'And we have Sarah.' She wasn't exactly crying; my sense was she was trying not to. But her voice trembled. 'She's so beautiful, Dev.'

'And so are you, Erin.'

Now the tears came gently, softly. 'Would you fly out for my operation so we can be together, like a family?'

'Of course I will.'

I sensed a smile through the snuffling. 'Andy.'

'What?'

'He told you I'd ask you, didn't he? Otherwise you wouldn't have answered so quickly.'

'Will this get him in trouble? I gave him my Boy Scout pledge.'

Another giggle. 'You and your stupid Boy Scout pledge. You're still using that after all these years?'

'Yeah, it's probably time I got some new material.'

'I know you like Andy. You try not to and I don't blame you in some ways. He's just so damned *nice*. And it's not put on. It's how he really is. He cares about people and he really cares about me. Sarah tried to resist him at first but he finally won her over.'

Sarah had indeed resisted him. She'd supported her mother divorcing me but she was suspicious of Andy for the very reason

Erin had fallen in love with him – he was so damned nice. Sarah hadn't believed it and neither had I, and so we'd commiserated and speculated about when he would reveal himself to be a monster. But even Sarah had succumbed to his decency and for a bitter time I'd felt that I'd lost both wife and daughter to him.

'I can't wait to see you, Dev.'

'Everything's going to be all right, you know.'

'That's what Andy says. He's very optimistic. But it is stage three. I'm scared, naturally. But with you and Sarah here – I still love you, Dev. I love Andy, too, but it's a different kind of love with him. I still love you so much.' Then, 'Just a few days till the three of us are together again.'

'I love you, Erin.' I smiled. 'I just wanted you to hear me say that.'

'You've made me laugh again. And you used my line.'

'I'll see you in a few days.'

'This has been wonderful, Dev. It really has.'

I sat there a long silent time afterward, a willing prisoner of the past.

'How much have you paid so far?'

'I'm trying to be pleasant about this,' Jeff Ward said. 'I wish I hadn't even mentioned it the other night. I've handled it.'

'What does that mean?'

'It means that when my father ordered me to let you come down here he meant for you to look over the campaign. And this has nothing to do with the campaign because I'm taking care of it on the side.'

'It has everything to do with the campaign and in other words you don't want me to know what the blackmailer's got on you or how much you've paid him or her.'

'It's none of your business. I was tired when I told you about it. I shouldn't have said a word.'

'I already know anyway.'

'What the hell are you talking about?'

My hotel room. Nearly five o'clock. Raindrops shimmied down the windows. Wind lashed the trees across the street. The congressman had complained that I didn't have the right to order him up here. I argued that this was the only safe place to talk. To that end I'd switched rooms. If anybody was planting bugs they were now one room behind.

We sat at a table overlooking the street that early dusk and rain had turned into gloom punctuated here and there with stoplights and neon. Green and red and yellow and the occasional ice blue for bars.

'I've seen the blackmail DVD, Ward. I take it you have, too.'

'Where the hell did you get hold of it?'

'Right now I'd rather not say.'

'You'd rather not say? You're working for me, remember?'

'No, I'm not. But I am trying to help you.'

He started rubbing his face with one hand and squeezing the beer bottle hard with his other. Rage and frustration rose from him like smoke from a machine that was about to explode.

'Did you recognize the woman on the video?' I said.

I had to let him sulk for a minute or so. 'I didn't actually see the video.'

'I don't understand.'

'I didn't see the video. I heard it. That's what he played for me.'

'Who's "he"?'

'How the hell do I know who "he" is? He's the 'he' who called me up and played the audio and said that this is from a video that they're willing to sell me for two hundred and fifty thousand dollars.'

'And you paid him?'

'Yes, I paid him.'

'And you got a copy of the video?'

'I didn't get dick. The bastard screwed me.'

'How long did it take for him to come back for more?'

'Do you know how smug you sound right now? You know everything, don't you, Conrad?'

'I got it from TV when I was about ten, Ward. Blackmailers always come back for more. That's rule number one. No genius involved in knowing that. So how long did it take?'

He swigged beer and then brought down his bottle like a judge gaveling down after he ordered a prisoner's death. 'One month. He wanted another two hundred and fifty thousand.'

'What did his voice sound like?'

'Electronic. Robot stuff. I'm only assuming it was a man. Could've been a woman the way they can do these things today.'

'The prostitute on the tape. Was she telling the truth?'

He moved around in his chair and his eyes avoided mine. He was uncomfortable now. 'Everybody has kinks. Everybody. Don't tell me you don't.'

'I probably do.'

'And she didn't have any problem with what we were doing when we were together those times.'

'Maybe because you were paying her. And maybe because she needed the money.'

'Yeah, well, whatever, she didn't say anything about it at the time.'

'She never said at any time that she'd rather not do those things?' Which is what she claimed on the DVD.

'Well, I suppose she did. But she's a whore. They all give you that shit from time to time. It's just a way of getting more money from you. "I'm doing this extra-special thing for you so would you do something extra-special nice for me?" And anyway, what are you, a voyeur? Why are we even discussing all this crap?'

'Because if this ever hits the press we'll have to refute everything she says on that tape point by point.'

He came up out of the chair as if he was going to dive at me which, at that moment, I wouldn't have minded. I'd slam his head against the table a few times and throw him the hell out and leave him to his fate. I just had to keep telling myself, *We can't lose this seat and let somebody like Burkhart win.* He was fine as long as you weren't of color, gay, poor, or held the protections of the Constitution near and dear. And not the so-called Constitution Burkhart and his followers had twisted into confirming all their prejudices.

'Maybe you're in on this whole thing, too.'

The stress was starting to make him paranoid.

I grabbed him by his famous black hair, then put the palm of my hand against his nose and shoved him backward as hard as I could. He hit the captain's chair with enough force to knock it over. He followed it down, still ranting.

I went and got myself another beer. By the time he got up he'd quit calling me names. I sat down and sipped at my beer and watched him.

'I'm calling my old man and you're gone – out the door, believe me.'

'You going to tell him about the hooker? Now get your ass back here. We're not done talking yet. And the next time you throw a tantrum I'm going to do what you want me to do – I'm going to make a reservation on the next plane out and leave you on your own.'

He had too much scorn and pride to admit that he didn't want me to do that. But with great dramatic reluctance he did upend the chair and come back and sit down.

'I'm trying to figure out how big the circle is – who else knows you're being blackmailed?'

He said it so casually I half wondered if it was a joke. 'My wife.'

'You told her everything?'

'I had to. She reamed my ass out of course for being with a hooker. She knows I run around but I usually stick with women who keep themselves clean. She's scared of AIDS. I had to tell her so she'd help me with the money drop. I couldn't ask anybody else on my staff to do it. I didn't want anybody else to know. And I just explained to her that if she didn't do it we wouldn't be going back to Washington, at least not in the congressional sense. I mean, I could always go to K Street. But being a congressman's wife has a lot of social perks.'

'She likes Washington, huh?'

'She comes from a very social family. Washington reminds her of how she grew up, I guess. I knew that if I told her I might lose the seat, she'd help me.' I didn't like his smile. 'I know how to handle her.'

To his credit he fought for all the right causes – and I believed he was sincere about them – but he was removed from the real world as most of us define it. His money and his mother-spoiling had made him more like a tourist than a resident. And it also sounded as if he'd married a woman just as vain and foolish as he was.

Then, by God, a whimper; a real whimper. 'Why the hell did David have to walk off now?'

In true sociopathic fashion, he just couldn't imagine why anybody whose wife he happened to be planking decided to leave the castle. 'You really don't see why he did it?'

'If you mean his wife – it was just a whim on both our parts. She'll straighten out. She's just got some kind of weird fixation on me. That kind of thing always passes. I tried to tell David that but he was too pissed to listen.'

There was no point in pursuing it, though now that he'd mentioned Nolan I wondered if there'd been any news about him. I asked Ward.

'He's probably getting drunk somewhere. He does that sometimes. He gets real down about something then disappears for two or three days. Ends up sleeping it off in some motel somewhere.'

'Tomorrow night's the debate. You going to be ready for it?'

'I thought you were only going to be here for two days.'

'I can always leave.'

'No, no – it's just – I know you're helping me. I have to admit that. But you're like my boss and that pisses me off. I don't like to be told what to do.'

'I'm making suggestions. You don't have to follow any of them. I'm not the "boss." You're the candidate. You make the final decisions.'

'I guess you're right.' He drank mightily of his brew. 'This is the first debate in my career where I won't have David at my side.'

'He's good.'

'If he'd just understand that it didn't mean anything to me.'

I wanted to laugh. Or smash his head in with a brick. Whichever came first. 'You know how stupid that sounds? You're sleeping with a man's wife and you're telling him that it doesn't mean anything. Now you're not only insulting him, you're insulting his wife as well.'

He shrugged. 'Maybe you're right. I know I'm not real sensitive sometimes.'

You have to look at these guys and wonder if they're of the same species you are.

'All right. I need to get to work and I'm sure you've got things to do. I want to start working on the source of this DVD. I'll keep you posted up until what time?'

'Around midnight. We usually watch one of the late shows in bed.'

'I probably won't have any news tonight but in case I do, leave your cell on.'

At the door, he said, 'I could really lose this, couldn't I?'

This was just now occurring to him? 'Not if we're smart.'

The grin belonged to a younger man. A more decent one. 'That's exactly what David would say. He's never let me down.'

I just nodded. I was sick of him and sick of myself for being so pompous about him.

Twenty minutes later Kathy Tomlin called me.

'Have you been watching TV?'

'No. Been working.'

'Something's going on. Lucy and I always keep monitoring the stations and Channel News Update just claimed that tonight at ten they'll have an important story about one of the candidates in this congressional race. Have you talked to Jeff?'

'He was here until just before seven.'

'And he didn't say anything about this?'

'No. And he would've. We went over a lot of things. I'm sure he doesn't know anything about this.'

'Well, he doesn't pay attention a lot of times. David always does that for him.' Lucy said something in the background. 'Lucy and I have a terrible feeling about this.'

'Tell her so do I.'

'Is there anything we can do?'

'See if you can get anybody at the station to tell you what the story is. You know anybody there well enough?'

'I knew one of the sports reporters in college.'

'There you go.'

'I don't know how he feels about me. I kept turning him down for dates.'

'It's worth a shot.'

'Lucy is waving hi.'

'I'm waving hi right back.'

'Are you really?'

'Pretty much.'

I still didn't have the name of the private investigator. I'd tried Nan Talbot's cell phone and her work phone and her e-mail but couldn't get a response.

I was more worried than I'd let on about this ten o'clock announcement. In a Florida district once Sylvia Fordham had pulled this same stunt. She'd managed to get herself a live interview on a ten o'clock newscast. She'd accused the opponent of a dalliance with one of his office women who'd proved to be an illegal immigrant of Hispanic extraction. Sylvia gave good TV. Her man had been three points behind when that little red light went on and she started talking. Same time next night, polling indicated that they were one point behind – inside the margin of error, of course.

I was surprised by how accessible she was.

'I thought you'd wait to congratulate me until after the ten o'clock show, Dev.'

'I'm calling to tell you you're making a big mistake and that you don't know what the hell you're dealing with, Sylvia.'

'Right. So we're going to blow your man out of the water and I'm making a big mistake?'

'You're at headquarters. That's only six or seven blocks from my hotel, the Royale. Get over here fast.'

'I'm not sure if we should start sleeping together, Dev. We might start talking in our sleep and give things away.'

'Knock off the bullshit, Sylvia. You know me and I know you. We don't like each other but we've both been in the same game for a long time. I know when you're serious and you know when I'm serious. Now I'm telling you that there's something you need to know before you go on that newscast tonight.'

'What the fuck are you talking about, Conrad?'

'My room is 538. I just took it. There's no possibility it's bugged. Get here as soon as you can.' I clicked off.

Nan Talbot didn't e-mail me. She phoned.

'God, I'm sorry this has taken so long. I got stuck in this city council meeting because the reporter who usually gets stuck with this stuff is covering a basketball game. I hate sports so I told him I'd cover for him. Anyway, I apologize and I've got that private investigator's name for you. You got a pencil?'

'Ready.'

'Lyle Gaskill.'

'Lyle Gaskill. You got anything more on him?'

'Just a cell number. I tried it. No longer in service.'

'Well, this is a good start. I really appreciate it.'

'Sorry I couldn't get back to you sooner. Say hi to Lucy. Remind her we've got a guy for her.'

'The Nan Talbot Dating Service.'

'Now that isn't a bad idea.'

'Thanks again.'

Not only was private eye Lyle Gaskill's cell phone out of service, so was he. I Googled him and found that forty-six-year-old Lyle Clancy Gaskill from Chicago had died five months ago of an aneurysm. He had been stricken while playing with his three children in his backyard and rushed to a hospital where he died later that night.

FIFTEEN

Sylvia always used it to her advantage, those sweet, earnest looks and that teenage slenderness. Would this gentle woman ever tell a lie? She brought with her night, chill, rain, and the unmistakable welcome scent of woman.

'None of your bullshit, Dev. I want to know what the hell's going on. I wanted to be with Rusty tonight. This is a big rally for him. We're all set to slap you down once and for all and put that pussy hound you represent out of business for good.'

'Jeff turn you down, did he?'

She snorted. 'Believe it or not, I turned *him* down one night a few years back. This was before I signed on with Rusty. We were at a Washington party. His dear little wife was sucking up to all the important people in the room, as usual. By now she must be wondering why she never gets invited to lunch. She's beautiful but so are a lot of climbers in Washington. So she's strictly B-list but she doesn't know it yet.'

'Thanks for that update, Sylvia. You want a drink?'

'What've you got?'

'Beer or bourbon.'

'Bourbon. And some water.'

'Sit down at the table. I'll turn the screen around so we can watch it together.'

'I race over here and you're offering me drinks. Where's the urgency?'

I made her the drink and brought it back to her. Then I went to the TV. The DVD was already loaded. I stood next to the screen with the remote. 'This is what you're going to break on the ten o'clock news tonight.' I clicked play.

I didn't watch the screen, I watched her face. And a fine patrician face it was, too. She disappointed me. She selected a mask of indifference and left it on for the length of the interview with the prostitute who enumerated all the ways that our congressman was a kinky devil.

I stopped the DVD after the segment about Jeff Ward.

'I'm curious about where you got *your* copy, Dev, but not all that curious. It's a *fait accompli*. We preview ten seconds of it tonight at ten. Of our copy, I mean. At least you and Ward won't be shocked.'

'In most circumstances this would be a game changer.'

She sipped her drink and made a face. Then she pointed a long royal finger at the glass. 'The urine of homeless people?'

'Such a delicate flower.'

'You really need to spend more than a dollar ninety-eight when you buy a half gallon of bourbon, Dev. Now what's this bullshit about "most circumstances"?'

'Just sit there, delicate flower, and watch.'

I hit play again. On came the woman who claimed that Rusty Burkhart, family values Burkhart, had not only visited her on many occasions but had also beaten her on three of them. She showed photos of the condition he'd left her in.

No mask this time. This was the real Sylvia Fordham. She was on her feet with the first mention of her client's name. She kept walking closer, closer to the screen. When the Burkhart segment finished, she dropped her head to her chest and stayed silent for several seconds. 'You bastard.' She walked back to the table and sat down. Her gaze was elsewhere. She was making all the same calculations I would have in her situation. 'Somebody was playing both sides.'

'Looks that way.'

'I knew Rusty was having some kind of trouble but he wouldn't tell me anything about it. He just kept saying it didn't have anything to do with the campaign.'

Burkhart was smart; even though she was working for him at the moment, he wouldn't want anybody as treacherous as Sylvia to know he was being blackmailed. You could never be sure what she'd do later on with the information.

'He's being blackmailed. The same as Jeff Ward.'

'Who the hell's behind it?'

'I don't know.'

'And of course you won't tell me how you got hold of it.'

'Not yet. Not until I know a lot more. And of course you won't tell me how *you* came by yours of Ward.'

'One of the nice things about being a national figure known for digging up dirt is that people offer you things you wouldn't know about otherwise. A private detective in Chicago offered it to me for a pretty hefty amount of money. Naturally, I couldn't say no. He didn't bother to tell me where he got it, and I don't care.'

'You need to make a decision here, Sylvia. If you go on with the Ward segment at ten o'clock, tomorrow morning I go to a local TV station and play the Burkhart for them.'

'All Burkhart did was push her around a little.'

'She says it was more. And anyway, Burkhart is God's man in the race. What's he doing in a whorehouse?'

She reached down. The sound of her purse opening. The sound of her digging around. Her fashionable hand appeared holding a package of fashionable French cigarettes and a lighter. 'Don't give me any bullshit about not smoking.'

'If the hotel sends me a bill, I'll send it to you.'

'Are you trying to scare me, Dev?'

'Not about smoking. But about going on at ten, I am. This is the kind of war that isn't going to do either side any good.'

'Afraid we're going to kick your ass with your wandering boy?'

I sat back in the captain's chair and watched her light her cigarette. 'You really want to risk it, Sylvia?'

'I'm not afraid of you, Dev. You should know that by now.' She exhaled a trail of blue smoke. How beautiful cancer is in a certain light.

'And I'm not afraid of you. So if you're going to the studio, you'd probably better get going. I've got other things to do.'

A hint of alarm in the eyes. 'So I just walk out of here?'

'You just walk out of here.'

'What changed your mind?'

'You did. I thought I could make you see that this DVD is a wild card for both of us. What the military calls unintended consequences. You blow something up and you're never sure what's going to happen afterward. We're blowing something up here, Sylvia. Maybe it'll be to your advantage, I don't know. But then it could also be to Ward's. I guess we'll just have to see.'

She managed a laugh while she sipped her drink. 'You're doing this very well, Dev. You're a good poker player. But I know you're bluffing. You're terrified of me going on TV tonight. We'll be on the air first with our story. And first matters in a case like this.' The shrewd, professional gaze. 'By the time I get to the door over there you'll be on your phone. Pure panic. I'd be the same way.' She sipped her drink. 'Sorry your bluff didn't work, Dev. But it was a good bit – how much we both have to lose if I go on tonight. You're good, but not that good, dear.'

But I was tired of it. Tired of her. Tired of the game. Tired of me. 'You talk too much, Sylvia. So do I, for that matter. I appreciate you coming up here. I still think you're making a mistake, but maybe not. I think this election should be about what kind of government we need. Burkhart's a racist and couldn't care less about anybody who isn't rich and powerful. We both know what kind of man Ward is. We're not talking about angels here. But at least Ward votes the right way.'

'I'm glad I brought a lot of Kleenex.'

'I guess the public'll just have to decide which is worse – a kinky congressman or somebody who beats up hookers.'

She gathered herself and stood up. 'We have one interest in common, Dev. We both want to find out who's behind this blackmail.'

'I agree.'

She moved to the door in a graceful sweep. 'Watch me at ten o'clock. This'll go national, Dev. My price'll go up even higher. Maybe someday you'll come to work for me.'

After she left I called Lucy and asked her to get Kathy so the three of us could talk. For once I appreciated the tinny music designed to make my wait more pleasant. I was on an elevator. I was going up and up and up to a better place. Any place but this one would be a better place at the moment. Then I heard Kathy say 'Dev?' and my elevator crashed back to reality.

'I'm back,' Lucy said.

'Sylvia Fordham and I tried to come to an agreement about her ten o'clock interview. She's going through with it so expect all hell to break loose. We need to get Ward and his wife ready for the cameras tomorrow morning.'

'What's going on, Dev?' Kathy asked.

'I can't discuss it on the phone.'

'This pisses me off, Dev. We have a right to know.'

'Yes, you do. But now's not the time.'

'You really want his wife?' Lucy said, trying to forestall Kathy coming back on me. 'That always looks so cruel. They just stand there suffering.'

'I don't want to send him out there alone. I don't like it either, but we don't have any choice. Neither of their daughters, though.'

'I saw some internals that just came in,' Kathy said. 'We're up with blue-collar voters. Burkhart's rant against unions pissed off a lot of working people. And now we have to deal with this – which you won't tell us about.'

'And this thing with Sylvia is all the press'll ask him about tomorrow night at the debate, too,' Lucy said. 'Where did this come from?'

'I'm not sure yet. I'm working on that part of it. But I'll need everybody on the upstairs staff to come in at seven thirty tomorrow morning. We'll do the press conference inside because the weather keeps changing. I want to make it look good for the video. I also want to pick the most photogenic of the volunteers to be on the sides of Ward so when the camera goes wide you see mature, attractive faces. You know Joan Rosenberg. She's a sweetie and she looks it. We'll definitely use her. We'll also need to get hold of a caterer first thing in the morning and have them rush brunch food and three or four big pots of coffee to us. Between you two, figure out which reporters will be civil to him. I want him to choose them for the first few questions. If there's national press he'll just have to punt.'

'I just hope we can pull all this off,' Kathy said.

'We will because we have to. If we can manage to get some sleep tonight things'll straighten out in the morning. I'd really appreciate your help on this, so if you come up with any ideas we'll talk about them first thing tomorrow.'

'I can hear that bitch cackling as soon as the camera's off her,' Lucy said.

'I take it the bitch you're talking about is Sylvia Fordham.'

'This is just the kind of thing she loves to do,' Kathy said.

I disliked keeping the information about Burkhart and all the rest from them, but right now I couldn't afford to trust anybody. First I needed to tell Ward about the other part of the DVD and how one part cancelled out the other in terms of usefulness. If we went after Burkhart with our part he'd come right back at us with his.

'Thanks for your help, both of you. All we can do is try. And make sure to get some sleep.'

'If I watch at ten I'll never get to sleep,' Kathy said.

'Me, either,' Lucy said.

'Then don't watch.'

'Listen to him,' Lucy said, 'like I suppose *you* won't watch.'

'Of course I'll watch. But right after that I'll guzzle down two quarts of vodka and I'll go right to sleep.'

It was now 8:40. A paralysis had set in. I should have gone downstairs to the bar and had a few and talked to some people. Just get my head back into the flow of normal life. But I was trapped up here and I knew it. I kept glancing at a dark TV screen the way I'd glance at my monitor after having a heart attack. Oh, she'd preen; oh, she'd swoon, our Sylvia. The sweet, proper girl.

Whatever happened to morality in this country? How can we expect to remain the best country in the history of man when we have leaders who violate the basic principles of family values? How can we keep returning to Washington the kind of man who disgraces the district he comes from?

I was pretty sure I knew how she'd handle the Burkhart part of the DVD. The only thing she could do. Reference it tonight and claim that Ward's side had seen the tape with the prostitute detailing his kinky ways and they right away created a fake tape to accuse Burkhart of the same thing. She would warn the true believers not to believe a second of it. She would say – and here she would sound almost melancholy – that she missed the days when this country didn't have to endure the kind of lies and nastiness that were part and parcel of so many campaigns these days.

Reporters would giggle, the not-news network would play sound bites of her rant for the next two news cycles and people in bars would get into loud arguments about the veracity of the Burkhart tape.

It was now 8:49.

When the phone rang I was grateful. Something to distract me from the dark TV screen.

'I'm calling from a phone booth.' Ward sounded as if a bully had just stolen his ice cream.

'Before we get started, I want to tell you something.' I explained to him about how the blackmail DVD was now useless to both candidates because there was video proving that both of them had gone to the same whorehouse. 'That's pretty good news.'

'You think so, Dev? You fucking think so? It's all coming down on me. Big time.'

God, I hated it when Ward whined.

My stomach knotted when he said, 'It's Bryn Nolan.'

'What about her?'

'She called and talked to Kathy a few minutes ago. She said she's going to the police right away to file a missing persons. And this on top of that snake Sylvia going on TV—'

He'd convinced Bryn Nolan to hold off reporting David's disappearance for a few days; the assumption being that David was trying to drink away the rage and sorrow he felt after learning about Ward and Bryn. If she called the police, the press would have the story within five minutes. When your key man goes missing you have a big problem, especially when one of your other employees was murdered in your headquarters' parking lot. I couldn't complain about Ward whining. I wanted to whine myself.

'You have to talk to her, Dev. You have to convince her to wait.'

'I've never even met the woman. Why would she listen to me?'

'She's heard good things about you. From David. He was the only one who liked the idea of bringing you down here. The rest of them were threatened.'

'Why now? What changed her mind?'

'I guess her two little daughters. They keep asking about their father. She's getting scared that maybe something happened to him. You know, the way it happened to Jim Waters.'

'Well, I suppose I can give her a call.'

'No!' he said. 'No, not a call. You have to see her in person. The phone won't cut it.'

'What the hell are you talking about? I need to be here at ten when the news comes on. We need an angle so we can respond.'

'This isn't a big city. She's maybe twenty, twenty-five minutes away. I can give you the address. Hell, you can watch the news there. She'll appreciate the company. She's going crazy and she doesn't think I'm a help at all.'

'I really resent this, Ward.'

'I don't blame you.'

'You don't blame me but you still want me to do it.'

'I'm desperate. You bought in, too – so now we're both desperate.'

I took down the address. Of course. And then went down to my rental. Of course. And set out in the dark rainy night. Of course.

PART THREE

SIXTEEN

Bryn Nolan wasn't as highly lacquered as Mrs Burkhart. She didn't need to be. She was a tall, preppy blonde with one of those freckled upper-class faces that you find in an F. Scott Fitzgerald. She wasn't quite a beauty but her face was so urgently pretty that she drew you in without any tricks. Gatsby would have invited her to any number of his parties.

She wore a dark brown sweater and a tweed skirt and a frown. 'This was so stupid of Jeff, Mr Conrad. I've already made up my mind. I'm sorry he made you make the trip.' She was as jittery as a junkie in need of needle love.

'So I should just go back to my car and get out of here?' Pity has never worked well for me. But I keep trying.

'Oh, Lord.' She flung a welcoming arm out. 'Please come in. At least let me pour you some coffee. David loves my coffee. Says it's the best he's ever had.'

She said all this to my back as I entered a small vestibule and turned left into a large living room at the suggestion of one more arm fling. The good taste assaulted me. This woman or her decorator had contrived a room that was imperious in its perfect harmony. Stone fireplace, Persian rugs, enormous couch, small sofa, love seat, and hardwood coffee table. Not necessarily all that expensive but not a single element that would upset a snob. Unlike my apartment in Chicago, there wasn't a stray sock or shirt to be found anywhere.

The fire was as appealing as she was. I sat in a leather chair staring into the flames. My mind was so overloaded it refused to deal with any of the problems at hand. It just roamed around image to image, mostly related to other fireplaces that had figured in my life. I thought of my ex-wife and of our daughter, of a girl I'd loved in high school, and of a cabin I'd rented once that had made me feel like a pioneer – until I'd had to use the outhouse in the middle of a snowy night.

'Here. I'm sorry it took so long.'

She was breathless; a few seconds away from hysteria. I took the saucer and cup she handed me. She went over and parked herself primly on the couch. She folded her hands as if in prayer and then loosed them like fluttering doves.

'You need to calm down, Mrs Nolan.'

'I know; I know. This is all my fault. All of it. If I hadn't been so stupid . . .' Her hands returned to prayer. 'I'm thirty-six years old and I feel like a college slut or something. Really. I even went to Confession. He was one of those new priests who "understands." I wanted the old-fashioned kind.' She had a smile that could start wars. 'You know, some big old monsignor who'd come over to your side and drag you out of the confessional and then start yelling at you in front of everybody else.'

'Well, if you find a church like that, let me know. I'd like to go there.'

The joke landed about thirty seconds after I sent it.

'Oh – right. You're kidding. God, I'm so scattered I can't think straight. I keep thinking David's dead.' Then, 'I wish I could tell you it wasn't exciting. It was. He made me feel alive again instead of like some dreary housewife. Jeff's very good at that. He got me to the point where I'd come to him any time of night or day. I was ashamed of myself but I couldn't stop. It was so high school. And then one day one of our daughters started screaming about something so I ran downstairs to see what was wrong. Jeff had sent me a kind of sexy letter and I was writing him back sort of a sexy one myself. I thought it was kind of a goof. I didn't close my computer. And I forgot about it because Chrissie had fallen on the driveway and had a cut on her head. When David found the letter he exploded, even though I told him it didn't mean anything.'

So Ward was telling poor Nolan that it didn't mean anything and his wife was telling Nolan that it didn't mean anything – apparently the only person it meant anything to was Nolan himself.

'He's a bender drinker,' I said. I wasn't in the mood to play a righteous monsignor. I wanted to find out where the hell her husband was.

'Yes. He goes to AA meetings twice a month.'

'So it is a definite possibility he's trying to drink through this.'

'Yes. But after what happened to poor Jim—'

'Does he ever call you when he's on one of his benders?'

'Not usually.'

'Does he tend to go to the same places?'

'He says not. Sometimes he goes into Chicago. A lot of the time he's not even sure where he went. He has to reconstruct his trips with credit card receipts.'

We fell into one of those uncomfortable silences that neither of us had the ingenuity to break. The phone rang and she leapt for it with Olympian zeal and prowess. It was on an end table. She probably could have picked up the entire table with her crazed strength.

'The Nolan residence.' Then: 'Oh, God, no, listen – I don't want to take a survey now and why the hell are you calling me at nine twenty? The cut-off's supposed to be nine o'clock!' She slammed the receiver down so hard I thought I heard the phone groan.

She touched long fingers to her perfect right breast. A hint of nipple made her all the more fetching. 'Now I know how people get heart attacks. Every time the phone rings my mind just explodes. And then my heart does, too.'

She came back and sat down. Her very nice legs were set exquisitely together. 'What were we saying?'

'I was wondering why you wanted to call in a missing persons report now?'

'Oh, yes. Of course. Because I'm having nightmares. I studied medieval English literature in college. Nightmares figured in a lot of the plays. They foreshadowed what was to come. We do some of that today. Look at all the paranormal shows on TV.'

'So you've been having nightmares about your husband.'

'As soon as I close my eyes they start. He's usually trapped somewhere – buried alive – or on an elevator – or in the trunk of a car – and he's always crying out for me to help him. He never talks about how I betrayed him. He doesn't have to. It's all I think about. Over and over and over. God, I wish I'd never met Jeff Ward.'

Sometimes the greatest mystery of all is the mystery of ourselves. We do something so out of character that we spend years trying to understand it and never do. Sometimes it's the liquor and sometimes it's simply some dark and deranged impulse. We go back and back to it as if to a great library in search of the one book that will explain it. But that book is always checked out.

'And you know what's so funny? I'm the jealous one in our marriage. I'm always worried some other woman will steal him away. I cringe every time I see him around Kathy Tomlin, for instance. Even when

I know it's business, when he's sitting with a reporter talking and she's wearing a skirt that barely covers her. I even got jealous one day when I saw him having coffee or something with Mrs Burkhart. At least I don't accuse him as much as I used to. My first true love cheated on me all the time. I've never trusted men since.'

Nothing to say to that. She was talking to herself, not me. I checked my watch. Eight minutes to go. 'We're in a lot of trouble. Could you at least hold off calling the police for twenty-four hours?'

'What if he's lying somewhere half dead?'

'We don't know that.'

'That doesn't mean it's not true.'

'All we can go on is past behavior.'

'I don't want him to die without saying he forgives me.'

Selfish, even narcissistic, but understandably human. She loved him and betrayed him and that was bad enough. But for him to pass on without there being some resolution—

'I understand, Mrs Nolan.' I was a mere human, too, and I did understand the need for absolution, pitiful as that was.

'Mrs Nolan. I have a first name, for God's sake.'

'All right, Bryn. I understand, but I still have to ask you to hold off for at least twenty-four hours.'

'You're all the same.' She shook her head angrily, a quite pretty child feeling sorry for herself. 'As loving as David is, he can be the same way. So callous when it comes to politics. Winning is everything.'

'Is it all right if we watch TV now?'

'What? Oh, right, Sylvia's on. God, I hate that bitch. She'll say anything.'

She was up again. 'Family room,' she said, and led us to a door with stairs that ended in a voluptuously furnished room complete with bar, gigantic plasma TV, pool table, and carpeting so thick you could lose your shoes in it.

We waited through six thirty-second commercials, two of them for Burkhart, before the local Ken and Barbie came on and sounded as urgent as possible about several of the headline stories.

Then Ken said, 'But we begin tonight with a visit from somebody who's frequently in the national news.' The camera widened out to a two-shot. Sylvia wore a white silk blouse and the same dark chignon that Audrey Hepburn had worn in numerous movies. Subtle sex. Cameras had always lusted after her and tonight was no exception. But what was that in her eyes? The expression I'd expected would have been joy, trashing and thrashing us with Ward's infidelity and kinky ways. But Sylvia's dark eyes were furtive; she was scared. And Sylvia was never scared.

'Sylvia Fordham is legendary in the business of politics. She is considered one of the toughest, if not *the* toughest, of all the political operatives in our country. She's working for the Rusty Burkhart campaign in our district and she's here tonight to tell us some things she says she's learned about Mr Burkhart's opponent, Congressman Jeff Ward.' Ken gave her his Ken smile. 'Would you like to make some news tonight, Sylvia?'

'I certainly would, Chad.'

'Something's wrong with her,' Bryn said.

'Yeah. For sure.'

She licked her lips and swallowed hard before starting to speak. 'Our campaign has learned that the state attorney general's office might finally look into some possible discrepancies in Congressman Ward's PAC reporting. He may not have reported everything during the last election cycle.'

'What the hell?' I said.

Ken blinked a couple of times. The magical coach had turned into a pumpkin and the beautiful maiden into a gnarled hag. This was the freaking big story they were breaking tonight? Some bullshit little routine accusation about PAC contributions – and in the last election cycle, for God's sake? If they had a mean TV columnist in this town, Ken and Company were going to get worked over big time for spending all night pushing the big reveal only to see it turn into nothing more than carping.

'I see. But I guess I need to ask if Mr Burkhart didn't already bring this up at the start of the campaign?'

'Yes, he did. But we think it's worth mentioning again now that the attorney general's office said they might look into it.'

Ken was less of a Ken than I'd thought. 'But the election commission has already looked into this and said that there's nothing improper in the filing. And you keep saying that the attorney general's office *might* look into it.' A quick smile. The contempt in it was blade sharp. 'I doubt Congressman Ward's going to lose any sleep over this tonight.'

A hint of professional sympathy stirred in my racing mind. Their plans had changed quickly. They weren't going to mention the DVD. But Sylvia had to go on anyway. She'd once staged a car accident to get out of an interview, but there hadn't been time for that tonight. So here she was on the tube with a story so lame even the news reader was mocking her. Knowing Sylvia, she'd want to get her hands on his scrawny neck and dispatch him on live TV. Which would have been a hell of a lot more interesting than what she'd done so far.

'Well, I know we have a lot of viewers watching tonight to see what kind of charges you wanted to unveil. I'm sure they understand the implications of this claim and I'm sure they'll be eager to learn more about the story as the election draws closer. Thanks very much for coming on, Miss Fordham.'

She was a trouper. She found a radiant smile for a closer and she shook his hand as if they'd just agreed on a pact to end poverty, all wars, cancer, and make prime-time TV more fun to watch.

'This is what Jeff was so nervous about?' Bryn asked, clicking off the picture.

'Either Sylvia changed her mind or somebody changed it for her. Maybe Burkhart himself.'

'But why would Burkhart stop her?'

'I'm not sure. Maybe it was as simple as deciding to hold it till closer to the election. It could have been any number of things.' My mind was already out the door. My body followed soon after. 'All I can ask you is to hold off calling the police until you hear from me tomorrow. Right now I need to find out what's going on.'

As I stepped over the threshold she grabbed the back of my arm. 'Tomorrow's the night of the debate. If I do it then I'd be betraying David. As much as he hates Jeff, he believes in defeating Burkhart.' She got all junkie jittery again. 'God, why did I sleep with him?'

I left her alone with the nasty night. And that miserable question she'd be asking herself for a long time to come.

SEVENTEEN

The parking lot glistened with slick pavement. Dirty moonlight and tumbling trash, like something out of a noir sci-fi film. Both Lucy and Kathy were in David Nolan's office when I got back. Each had a bottled wine cooler in front of her. They didn't seem to be in danger of becoming rummies anytime soon.

'We don't know whether to celebrate or not,' Kathy said.

'We just wish we knew what was going on,' Lucy said.

'Well, at least we won't have to be in at seven thirty,' I said. 'No reason to have a news conference.'

'That doesn't clear things up,' Lucy said.

They still hadn't been told about the DVD and I wasn't going to be the one who broke it to them. 'There's beer in the fridge down the hall, Dev. That's where Kathy found the wine coolers.'

I went and got one and came back. 'Right now all we can do is concentrate on the debate tomorrow night.'

'Jeff was crazy tonight. He said there was going to be this big explosion after Sylvia went on TV. But it was nothing.' I watched Kathy's lips. She had an interesting way of applying them to the neck of the bottle. Very neat and tidy. Almost chaste. Fascinating.

'Well, for whatever reason, it didn't happen.' I twisted the cap off my beer. 'I assume Jeff and I can get into the auditorium in the afternoon and check everything out.'

They glanced at each other, still not happy that I was keeping information from them. But they were pros and acted like it.

'They said two o'clock to three o'clock,' Lucy said.

'It's a good venue,' Kathy said. 'Great acoustics. Jeff has had three debates there over the years. He's comfortable there.'

'You have any video of Burkhart debating, Kathy?'

Two minutes later Kathy handed me a DVD marked Burkhart vs. Steinem. The date was three years ago. 'This was from the primary when he was running for governor. Some amazing stuff in there.'

I went over to the video rig and set things in motion. I punched play. The forty-inch plasma TV bloomed. The first image told me that I was looking at a home video. Not a bad home video but a home video nonetheless.

Whoever had shot it must have come late because the first audio belonged to then-Congressman Norm Steinem and he was already in the middle of a sentence.

'—at California. Look at the trouble they're having with all their anti-tax legislation. The state government is paralyzed. It's virtually impossible to raise taxes when it's necessary. And sometimes it is necessary. We need government services and sometimes that means taxes.'

The camera panned over to Burkhart while Steinem was talking. He looked uncomfortable in a suit and tie. His toupee was cartoon red. The way he gripped the podium suggested he might crush it sometime soon. He knew how to steal a scene. As Steinem spoke Burkhart winked at his supporters, rolled his eyes once and then put a finger gun to his head at the mention of taxes and pulled the trigger. The laughter from his side of the auditorium was loud. The moderator who sat between the two podiums appeared most unhappy.

'Mr Burkhart, I thought we agreed that you wouldn't pull any of the stunts you did in the first debate.'

Burkhart loved it. He pointed to himself, grinned to his people and said, 'I'm a bad boy.' Then: 'I apologize to you and I apologize to Mr Steinem. I just enjoy having some fun. But I can see that this isn't the time or place for it.'

Everybody in the house was waiting for the punch line but it never came. The debate settled into sonorous titting and tatting.

It was eighteen minutes and thirty-six seconds before Burkhart let Burkhart become Burkhart, when it was his turn to respond to a question on prayer in school. Then he riffed, then he wailed, a born-again jazz man sending his lumpen messages out to true believers everywhere.

'You know why I wear this little American flag pin? You know what it symbolizes to me? It symbolizes the America I grew up in. Hard work and family church and belief in the finest country God ever created. And no matter how much they try to dirty and pervert this land of ours, this pin right here is my shield. It protects me and my family from the atheists and the degenerates and the global-warmers and the gay-pushers and the liberals who mock those of us who love our country and mean to save it. And prayer in school is one of those issues where I'm using my shield – and picking up my sword – to make sure that it's still allowed in schools everywhere. I pray to God every morning at my desk and I don't see anything wrong with our children doing the same thing. All we're asking is that we have the right to keep America the way it was – and the way it should still be!'

Maybe he wasn't Reagan but he was just close enough to make a solid impression. The physical heft, the hard face, the rich voice . . . he was corny but effective.

I watched the entire debate. I judged Burkhart the winner by a few points. What had cost him the election were all the stories about the lawsuits at the various companies he owned. Age discrimination, sex discrimination, unsafe working conditions, sexual harassment, and some video clips of him at a Chamber of Commerce meeting railing against the minimum wage. 'This is destroying the opportunity to offer Americans what they really want – more jobs.' Yes, at $1.25 an hour.

But all of this had failed to seriously damage Burkhart this time around. His flag pin speech was packing them in. He was still the odds-on winner of this campaign.

I walked the DVD down the hall to Kathy's desk.

'I'd vote for him,' I said.

'He's good on the stump. And he's not a moron. He's just a country-club bully who picked the right year to trot out all his bullshit again.'

'Other than that you're nuts about him.'

'I'm secretly in love with him.' She pointed to a chair. I sat. She planted her nice elbows on her desk and her face in the V of her hands and said, 'You really going to keep us in the dark?'

'I'm going to try to.'

'You don't trust us.'

'This really bother you or are you just having fun?'

She shrugged and sat back in her chair. 'A little of both, probably. Lucy and I have been with Jeff since the beginning. It kind of hurts our feelings that you come along and keep us out of the loop.'

'So it's me you're pissed at?'

'Pretty much.'

'Anything I could do to change that?'

She put a finger to her cheek and pretended to be pondering the question. 'How about buying me a drink and not putting the moves on me?'

EIGHTEEN

'The first congressman I worked for was in the late nineties. I was just out of college. I wrote his speeches and did the scheduling, even though I didn't have a clue about what I was doing. I really liked him for taking a chance on me until I found out he was doing all this so he could get me in bed. You know when you hear all these actresses complaining about how being beautiful is really a pain sometimes? Well, it really is. I'm pretty but I'm hardly beautiful. But just being pretty – and God, there are millions and millions of girls prettier than I am – even then it gets in the way. He wanted me to go back to Washington with him. Yeah, right.

'The second congressman was straight-ahead but he had this insanely jealous wife. She called me out at this party one night. Made this big scene about how I was destroying her marriage. This was in their home. One of their teenage daughters was on the stairs listening to it all. The story got into the press. I quit. Even the tabloids picked it up. There was the photo of the congressman and me on the front page right in the checkout lane. My poor parents. My dad's a doctor in a small town. It was humiliating for him. I kind've liked the congressman I'd been working for. I always felt that maybe we should have slept together after all. At least we would've gotten something out of it. He lost, of course. The scandal did him in. He's still married to that hysterical bitch and I'll never know why.

'The third congressman was straight-ahead, too. Good, bright family man who practiced what he preached. But the other side planted a spy in our camp. He started leaking stories to the media about the congressman and I having an affair. If I was a reporter I'd have believed him, too. He looked legitimate. He was a driver and he worked with the volunteers. By the time we figured out he was a plant he'd done some damage. The media had played with some hints and the hints had started to have an effect on the voters. Fortunately, we were able to win, anyway.

'Then Lucy called me about Jeff Ward. Everybody always thinks that I was a sorority girl or something in college. Actually, I was very shy. In high school I'd been fat and had a bad complexion. By sophomore year in college I'd sort of bloomed outwardly but inwardly I was still the same high school girl so I didn't hang around with any of the cliques. Lucy and I had two poly sci classes together and we became friends. I thought it'd be great to work with her so I joined the Ward campaign just under three years ago.'

She was as pleasant to listen to as she was to look at. The late hour and the drinks that brought on a melancholy kind of sexuality made me feel comfortable for the first time since I'd arrived in town. I could close my eyes and imagine myself back in Chicago in similar circumstances.

'I'm just afraid of what I'll turn into.'

'And what would that be?'

'Oh, one of those older women you see on the Sunday talk shows. Kind of coarsened by all the years of working on campaigns and being strident and adamant about things. There's always something sad about that. The men get to be gray-haired and wise even if they're morons but the women just look used up and kind of hysterical. And nobody really pays attention to them. They just have them on the shows because they need females for their demographic base.'

'So where will you go after Ward?'

'Not sure yet. Maybe try to find a small college somewhere and teach. I've got a master's in poly sci. I could work on a doctorate while I taught.'

'You wouldn't miss the fun?'

She frowned. 'Some fun. Jim gets murdered, nobody can find David, and Burkhart seems to have something on Ward. And Ward has really disappointed me. I'm thirty-four years old. I think it's time for a husband and a family, and the kind of guys you meet on the trail aren't exactly the right kind of material for domestic bliss. And since I've never been much for one-night stands, I get pretty lonely.'

I remembered her telling me not to put the moves on her. I wondered if I was that obvious. Probably. I was as lonely as she was and needful of bed. My mind was getting clouded with the one thought that banishes all other thoughts – sex.

'You're going to start glowing in the dark pretty soon,' she said.

'Pardon me?'

'You're starting to radiate.' She stretched out her arm and offered me her hand. I took it. 'Do you ever just sleep with a woman? No sex, I mean. Just sleep.'

'I've tried. It's a bitch.'

'At least you're honest.'

Then I realized how dumb I was. 'But I'd be willing to try. I'm pretty tired. Maybe I'd fall asleep right way and it wouldn't be any problem after all.'

I was a dog, tongue hanging out, begging for scraps.

'Now I sound like a tease. I'm sorry. But you were right in the first place. It's a bitch trying to just sleep. But I have this thing about one-night stands.' She glanced at her watch.

The crew was starting to close the hotel restaurant. They did so with great and pointed clamor. I didn't blame them. It was late and they wanted to go home.

Our hands parted. 'Maybe some other night, Dev. It's just all so crazy tonight.'

I wasn't quite sure what had distressed her so much. Given all the campaigns she'd worked on she'd certainly run into moments like those of seeing Sylvia Fordham on TV. Most modern campaigns depend on bombast and calculated revelations. And this revelation had been pulled at the last minute. Maybe it was the hour, the two drinks we'd had, or the simple fact that she decided I wasn't worth the trouble. So here I was near midnight, isolated again, even though a most fetching woman sat less than two feet from me.

She was out of the booth in seconds. 'I just need some sleep, Dev. But I've really enjoyed our talk.'

'Me, too.'

In my room I checked messages and e-mails. Tom Ward had written me an especially long message. He wanted to know if he should fly here and help out. He wouldn't ask any questions on the computer in case we were being monitored. But he used a kind of code to let me know that he had guessed that something big was about to break and that Sylvia Fordham pulling her punch was only a temporary break. He surmised correctly that she'd be back. Sylvia had the vampire gene. You couldn't kill her.

I wrote back, also in a kind of code, that I thought we could handle things here. Tom would just make things worse. He'd play father to Jeff's prodigal son and that would only complicate things all the more.

I needed three shots of whiskey to get to sleep. Not anything I wanted to depend on. Thoughts of my daughter and ex-wife came as I felt myself slipping into the soothing darkness. We'd been happy for the first four years. Even now I could smell the baby powder and the baby food and the wonderful scent of our daughter sleeping as my wife and I stood by her bassinet. I had never loved a woman as much as I did my wife in those days. Just thinking about my daughter could make me cry. But somehow I'd smashed it all.

I wanted to be standing next to that bassinet again with my arm around my wife and my tiny daughter sleeping with sweet and utter bliss.

But the dream gods were not kind to me tonight. I didn't remember the nightmares exactly, but in the morning I was depressed and frightened. I feared for beautiful Erin.

NINETEEN

Between the hours of eight fifteen and ten o'clock the next morning I followed Mrs Burkhart from her home. She went to a pricey restaurant, presumably for breakfast, and then drove to a mall. Since tailing her wasn't doing me much good I was ready to just go up to her in the parking lot of the mall, but there were too many people around. I could hear the news reader now: 'Eyewitnesses said that a political consultant from Congressman Jeff Ward's camp accosted Teresa Burkhart in a mall parking lot this morning. Teresa Burkhart is the wife of Rusty Burkhart, Congressman Ward's opponent in the upcoming election. Police are investigating.'

I didn't have any trouble finding her inside. The upscale stores were on the second level, east side. She was window-shopping.

She was assessing a display of winter coats. I walked up beside her. 'I like the belted one.'

She didn't look at me. 'You're stalking me.'

This morning she was dressed as a spy in her black Burberry and cute little faux fedora. She'd changed perfumes. This one had the same power of Eros as her previous one. She was worth every penny he spent on her.

She twisted around. Angry. 'What the hell do you want from me anyway?'

She said it with crowd-pleasing fury. Shoppers slowed to see what had so displeased the lady. Everybody loves a free show.

'Why don't we go have a cup of coffee, Mrs Burkhart? We need to have that talk.'

'Absolutely not.'

'Then I guess I'll have to call the police. I think I mentioned before that the police'll be interested in why you were taking photos of Jim Waters on the day he died. From a car. Without his permission.'

'Have you ever stopped to consider the possibility that I *had* his permission?'

'That's so stupid it's not worth answering. So what's it going to be – coffee or the cops?'

'I hate you.'

I began walking away. She was good. I got five stores down before she caught up with me. She'd shaken my confidence. I'd started to wonder if she was just going to let me walk away.

Neither of us spoke. We used the escalator. On the ground floor we found a restaurant open and went inside. The motif was medieval. I wondered if grog was on the menu.

I'd only had a piece of toast and coffee for breakfast so I ordered scrambled eggs and hash browns. The waitress kept glancing at Mrs Burkhart, who looked as if she was being held here against her will. When the waitress asked if there was anything she wanted, all Mrs Burkhart did was shake her head.

'I hate you.'

'I think the waitress heard you say that.' I wasn't joking. She'd said it when the waitress was only a few feet from our table, walking away.

'I don't care.'

'If somebody recognizes who you are, you'll care. Somebody'll let the media know that you were seen having coffee with a strange man. And that you might have been having a spat, a lovers' spat.'

It was bullshit but it worked.

'What the hell do you want from me?'

'The truth. Why you were taking photos of Waters.' I hesitated. 'And why you were seeing David Nolan?'

For a cunning woman, she wasn't much good at covering her feelings. She lurched as if somebody had jammed a knife blade into her side. Those rich dark eyes showed panic.

'I ran into him once. I thought it would be nice to sit down and talk to him. You know, to show that there were no hard feelings. Believe it or not, I like to be sociable. I get tired of all the name-calling.'

'You saw him on at least four other occasions and I've got proof of that.'

'That's a lie.'

And so it was. But again the way she responded – eyes averted now, faint sheen of sweat on her forehead, troubled breathing – I knew that my lie had evoked the truth.

'I need to go to the ladies' room.'

'No.'

'You can't stop me.'

'I want you to answer my questions before you do anything else. About Waters and about Nolan.'

'I'll answer when I come back.'

She was out of the booth before I could do anything. And what could I do anyway? Tackle her and drag her back? *Political consultant was arrested this morning for clubbing a helpless woman to prevent her from using the ladies' room.*

I tried hard to enjoy my breakfast. The eggs were delicious and the hash browns just the way I liked them. Mrs Burkhart was long gone, of course. The only thing I might have accomplished was scaring her into doing something that would reveal what was going on here.

Why had she been talking to David Nolan?

The Sandler College auditorium was a red brick building complete with a church-like steeple and a tree-lined walkway that led to campus. With the sun out and the trees blazing with autumn, I remembered how I'd imagined college life when I was small. I'd read a lot of adventure novels back then and colleges were usually depicted in the books as places where young geniuses met wise older professors who encouraged them to take on tasks that would somehow change the world – open doors to other dimensions, help create a species of super-humans, make contact with beings from other galaxies. But alas, college days, my college days anyway, were mostly about beer, girls, and studying. All of which was fine. But I still wished I'd stood on a hill one night and been contacted by another planet, the way John Carter had been in my favorite Edgar Rice Burroughs novel.

An army of TV people had taken over the auditorium. Miles of black cable, men and women pushing cameras around on stage, sound checks, lighting checks, rostrums being set in place, all for a night that would hopefully attract not only a large viewing audience but also a few headlines. Maybe even a career-destroying statement uttered in haste or anger. It was a boxing match with words.

I didn't see any of our people so I just dropped into a chair in back and opened my laptop and checked in with the home office. None of the internals had changed much. There was a *Tribune* poll that showed a tie, Burkhart with a one-point lead, but since that was well within the margin of error it was moot. My other candidates hadn't moved much either.

I went to HuffPo and Talking Points Memo for breaking news. A candidate in Texas wanted to declare all liberals 'enemies of the state,' and a congressman on our side was trying to explain why he'd hired five of his inexperienced relatives as staffers. The way of the world.

My cell phone beeped. I smiled as soon as I heard her voice. 'Are you in some important meeting?'

'Yes. The president and I are discussing whether or not to round up Goth people and make them start wearing real loud Bermuda shorts and yellow T-shirts.'

'Humorous. Just like my father.'

'But you don't like your father and I thought you were crazy about me.'

'Well, I like you better than my dad but that doesn't mean I trust you very much. No offense, but you're sort of out of it. In general, I mean.'

'Who could take offense at that?'

'I went back to Jimmy's apartment. My wallet must've fallen out when we climbed on to the fire escape. I had to be nice to that creep again. I even had to let him rub against my leg. He's like a dog.'

The colorful world of young Goths in America.

'So did you find your wallet?'

'Yeah. But that isn't why I called. He wanted to know who you really are. I guess he saw us standing at the bottom of the fire escape. I lied and said you were just this friend of mine. Then he started telling me that three or four nights before Jimmy died these two people came real late at night and went upstairs. He saw them because he had to help the old woman who lived across from Jimmy get her cat. The cat got out and was running around the apartment house.'

'Did he describe the two people?'

'He said they looked like rich people, but remember, anybody who takes a shower probably looks like they're rich to him.'

God, I liked her. 'He give you any details?'

'Yeah, but he was suspicious. He wondered why I was so interested. I told him because Jimmy was my friend and somebody murdered him. That's when I had to let him rub up against my leg.' She then started painting a verbal picture of Mrs Burkhart and David Nolan. And then she said, 'He said he almost went up there because he could hear them shouting at each other. But just when he was putting on his shirt to leave his apartment they quieted down. He said they probably stayed about half an hour.'

'Did he tell the police any of this?'

'He said he didn't tell the police anything they didn't ask. He said his best friend was doing time in Joliet and that even though he'd run over that chick he was a nice guy when he was sober and because of that he wouldn't tell the cops dick. That's the word he used, 'dick.' Does any of this help you?'

'A lot.'

'I miss Jimmy. He was my best friend, Dev.'

Rusty Burkhart strode on to the stage for the rehearsal. He had the easy, comfortable masculinity of the old Western movie stars. He shook enough hands to give himself blisters and then ambled over to one of the rostrums, hefty but not fat in his charcoal shirt and jeans. He'd once claimed he was from Viking blood, which was possibly true if Vikings had worn lurid red toupees.

Jeff Ward in the flesh appeared from the other side of the stage. I wondered if he'd coordinated his outfit with Burkhart. Blue shirt, jeans, Western boots. We weren't going to have a debate; we were going to have a hoedown.

Being pols they shook hands like old friends. Being in a photo op they smiled their asses off, too. And being single-minded about winning they started taking shots at each other with the smiles getting bigger and bigger.

Speaking to the small cadre of TV reporters and camera people standing on the floor below him, Rusty Burkhart produced some kind of document from his back pocket and waved it at them. 'We'll see if my friend Jeff here is willing to sign my "I Am an American" pledge tonight. That's one way we'll know if he's going to do right by this country or not. A lot of people are suspicious about anybody who won't sign this pledge. And by people I mean voters.'

They were like a vaudeville team. Now it was Ward's turn to shine. 'And while I'm not signing the pledge that violates many parts of our sacred Constitution, I will be reminding voters that my friend Rusty here once said that maybe God's plan was to have sick people die if they couldn't afford to pay for their own insurance. He hasn't been saying that much lately.' Ward was shaking his head like a schoolmarm who'd just uncovered a turd on the floor.

'Not only have I not been saying it lately – I've never said it.' So there. Burkhart sounded definite.

'But there's a tape of you saying it, Mr Burkhart,' a young female reporter said.

'Completely out of context. And let's not change the subject.' He waved his pledge again.

What we had here was similar to the weigh-in for a heavyweight champion boxing match. The fighters wanted a good crowd so they gnawed on the other guy's ass to the delight of the press.

The last thing I paid attention to was Ward saying, 'What Mr Burkhart is saying here is that if we got rid of the minimum wage we'd put a lot more people to work. But I don't know many folks who'd sweat and slave for a dollar an hour.'

'Nobody ever said anything about a dollar an hour and you know that, Congressman.'

And so on.

I went back to my work on my laptop. I didn't know much about David Nolan so I tried to find as many short biographies of him as I could. I had no idea what I was looking for. I had one fact to guide me. He and Ward had been best friends for most of their lives. And yet he and Mrs Burkhart had not only been together some of the time, they'd visited Jim Waters a few nights before his death. There was a connection here somewhere, but what was it?

I skimmed the results of numerous Google searches before hitting one from an alumni magazine piece that spotlighted Nolan and Ward as celebrated former students. The first five hundred words focused on the politics of their time in Washington, the second five hundred words dealt with their student council activities while undergrads at the school. It was in the final five hundred words that I found what I was looking for.

'Most reports about the friendship of the two men omit the year they didn't speak to each other. Even now they are reluctant to discuss it. This happened in 1993 according to some of their close friends. But even they aren't sure what caused the rift. What ended their disagreement – subject still unknown – was that they were seated near each other at a homecoming football game. Ward claims that Nolan came over to him and offered his hand; Nolan insists it was Ward who came over and offered *his* hand. Whatever, the friendship was renewed.'

Precedent. What had happened back then? And did it have any bearing on their recent falling-out?

By the time I was finished Burkhart and his people had left the stage. Ward stood by the podium he'd been assigned, talking to a member of the TV crew. As I walked over to them, Ward was pointing to a light placed directly above him. 'I'm not trying to tell you your job, Jason, I'm just saying why don't we light it up and take a look. I don't want to pull a Dick Nixon here. Remember the first Kennedy-Nixon TV debate?'

If Jason remembered reading about the debate, it hadn't made a big impression. He just shrugged. 'Congressman, I've been lighting these debates for years now. I think I know what I'm doing.'

'How about humoring me? How about setting the lights the way I want right now, then we'll tape me at the podium and look at it. Fair enough?'

Jason didn't even try to look happy. 'I guess so, Congressman. Why don't you go over and get in place, then, and I'll start lighting the stage.'

'I really appreciate it, Jason. You're a good man.'

As soon as Jason was out of hearing range, Ward said, 'That fucker has no idea what he's doing. I wanted to bring my own lighting man. But the old fart who oversees these debates said we had to use the same people. Burkhart doesn't care. He looks like a bear and people like him that way.'

'You'll look fine.' Then: 'Why did you and Nolan have a falling-out back in 1993?'

He'd been distracted by two men lugging the moderator's desk on stage. But when I spoke he whipped around and said, 'What the hell kind of question is that? I'm supposed to be prepping for a debate tonight, remember? Staying calm and focused. And you bring up some old nothing bullshit like that?'

We were starting to get an audience. His voice was high, strident.

'Keep your voice down. There're reporters here.' I spoke so only
he could hear. 'I just asked you a question.'

'Well, un-ask it. This isn't the time or place.'

Over the speaker Jason said: 'Congressman, would you take your
place at the podium, please.'

It was as if a starting pistol had been fired. Ward broke away and
walked double time to the stage. Nobody up there was going to ask
him any questions about why he and Nolan had not spoken for a
time back then. In fact, since this was only a rehearsal of sorts,
nobody was going to ask him any difficult questions of any kind.
He took his place behind the podium.

The smile and charm came with light-switch speed. The reporter
and her crew moved in for the same kind of shots they'd gotten
with Burkhart. Ward knew better than to try any diva routines about
the lighting. The press would love a story about his vanity. While
a good number of men probably envied his success with women,
there was something a bit unmanly about it when the cocksman
was wealthy and obviously pampered. A courtesan rather than a
warrior. That wasn't his problem alone. Senator John Kerry had
after all gone out and bought himself several thousand dollars' worth
of hunting gear for a photo op that made him look like a member
of Nerds Gone Wild. I'm told there is a photo somewhere of a rabbit
giving him the finger.

I was soon back at work on my laptop. I wanted to know more
about the rift between Ward and Nolan but Mother Google wasn't
yielding much. I switched over to my other campaigns. Updates.
Scuttlebutt. One of our candidates had been shouted down by two
men in an open meeting. Our campaign runner there was sure they
were hired to do so by none other than Sylvia Fordham herself,
who was running the opponent's campaign. She was sure she'd seen
these two at other open meetings.

She snuck in without me seeing her. But when I looked up there
she was, the back of her anyway, eight or nine rows ahead of me.
Mrs Teresa Burkhart. Her coiffure was unmistakable, as was the
way one of her husband's campaign staffers served her coffee – with
great trepidation if I interpreted her body language correctly. The
young woman turned out to be none other than Melanie, the pretty
teenager who'd tried to have me thrown out of Burkhart headquarters. I recognized her when she glanced my way. She recognized

me, too, and immediately bent to inform her employer of my presence.

After the soul-saver had left the side of Mrs Burkhart, but not before she scowled in my direction of course, I closed my laptop and traveled down the aisle. I seated myself directly behind Teresa Burkhart. The way her neck and shoulders tensed, I knew she was aware of me. I said nothing for a few minutes. Two or three times she started to turn around and face me then thought better of it.

'I see the most beautiful woman in the world sitting out there,' Burkhart boomed from his podium. He waved to his wife and sent her a bashful-boy grin.

She raised a fawn-colored glove and waved.

The man overseeing the debate, whom Ward had referred to as an 'old fart,' was a former governor from the other side named Will Carney. We should all look like such old farts as Carney did at seventy-eight or thereabouts. He crossed the stage briskly, a tall, slender man in a blue windbreaker, white shirt, chinos, and white Reeboks. He had a headful of curly silver locks that any Roman senator would have envied and a voice as imposing as a general's sounding the call to war. It was nice to see how much he intimidated the two candidates. He told them the kind of debate he wanted tonight; the kind, he said, 'they owed the public, given all the bullshit in the air this election cycle.' I took this to be criticism of some of the wilder and woolier candidates of his own party.

He had one major failing, did ex-Governor Will Carney, and the press and political cartoonists had always enjoyed bringing attention to it. Once he started talking he never wanted to stop. You needed ten armed guards to drag him off the stage. And he'd still be talking as they dragged him.

Today was no different. He got so intensely involved in talking about the kind of debate this state deserved – he'd been a pretty good governor: honest and inventive and willing to work with our side – that the initial surge of surprise and pleasure he'd brought with him now became weary resignation. When was this old fart ever going to shut up?

I decided now was as good a time as any.

'You're in a lot of trouble. And maybe I can help you. But I'm sick of chasing you around. You call me if you change your mind. But you don't have much time.'

I didn't give her a chance to say anything. I just stood up, my laptop under my arm, and started to walk out of the auditorium.

In the lobby a harried-looking Lucy Cummings was hanging up her coat. When she saw me she rushed over, breathless. 'God, I'm sorry I'm late. I had to set things up with this caterer for the party after the debate tonight. He wanted all this fancy food. I told him there'd be a cross section of people there so to keep it simple.' She crossed her eyes. I appreciated her making me laugh. It felt good. 'I think I offended him. He said that his clientele always wants sushi. I told him that most of the union guys would probably prefer little fried pieces of shrimp. He said maybe I should go to Red Lobster. Actually, that sounds pretty good to me. I love Red Lobster.' Then: 'God, here I am running my mouth off and Jeff's in there alone.' She touched my arm. 'Bye.'

TWENTY

When I got back to my hotel Sylvia Fordham was sitting in the lobby in her best Audrey Hepburn pose. The lovely naïf lost in a world of sensationalism and sin. The dress was a simple blue number that modestly revealed the slender but comely body. She sat on a couch reading the *National Review*. I curbed my desire to take a match and set it on fire.

She pretended not to notice me when I sat down next to her.

'You look very nice today, Sylvia. How about going upstairs with me?'

Her gaze rose from the magazine and settled on me. The smile was playful. 'I knew you'd come around someday. Even as much as you hate me.'

'I don't hate you, Sylvia. I just think you're a reprehensible threat to our republic.'

'Well, if that's all—' The smile remained.

'So what happened to last night's big announcement?'

'You feel like a drink?'

'It's early.'

'Then you get Kool-Aid or something. I'm having a drink.'

And so she did. We were tucked away in a booth in the hotel bar. It was dark enough to get lost in. You needed a coal miner's lighted hat to get around. The waitress appeared out of the gloom as if she'd stepped from another dimension. I had coffee and Sylvia had a double Scotch straight up. If I didn't know her, it would be easy to have one of those eight-hour crushes on her. She really was beautiful and quietly sexual.

'I can't believe this. Here I've got the best piece of evidence I've ever had against an opponent and I can't use it. This is really bullshit, Dev.'

'I can say the same, Sylvia. Remember that. But you haven't told me about last night.'

The waitress must have been wearing track shoes. She reappeared out of the vortex in what seemed like seconds. After she was gone again, Sylvia said, 'I'd usually go ahead on my own with something like this – I just assumed Rusty would be happy with taking Ward down this way. But when I went out to his place and told him about what I'd set up with the TV station he blew up at me. He finally told me the truth about the blackmail, how he was being shaken down the same way Ward was. He said absolutely no way did he want me to run the clip.' A sigh followed that Bette Davis would have considered too dramatic. 'When I write my memoirs I'm going to mention this incident as the most perfect takedown I ever had – and couldn't use.' Then: 'Now what I want to know, since we're sort of in this together, is who's blackmailing them?'

'I'm not sure. I'm beginning to suspect who but I don't want to say anything until I know more.'

'And you're still covering up the fact that Nolan's missing?'

'You've got spies everywhere.'

'Everywhere.'

'Was Jim Waters one of yours?'

'Wouldn't *you* like to know?'

'That means he wasn't.'

'If you say so.'

'This is like third grade.'

'I had a great time in third grade.'

She waved for another drink. 'The debate tonight should be interesting. They're both up there going through the motions when the only thing either of them wants to talk about is how the other guy went to this whorehouse all the time.'

I'd never known her to be giddy but she was close to it now. She was a killer but at least she had a sense of irony. I'll bet neither Hannibal nor Genghis Khan had a sense of irony.

After she sipped her freshener, she said, 'Our internals say we're neck and neck.'

'Same here. Margin of error.'

'Well, it's going to be interesting to see what you do next, Dev.'

'I'm sure you'll come up with something that'll degrade all the standards of taste and decency.'

'I'll try but doing it isn't as easy as it looks. I wish I was as much of a bitch as people think.' The way she was playing with her glass, twisting it around, I realized she was stalling. I'd wondered why she'd come to my hotel. I had pretty much surmised by now that Burkhart had been afraid to run the video of the prostitute talking about Ward because then Ward would run the video about Burkhart. It was nice that Sylvia had confirmed it for me but it was unlike her to be so friendly and offer so much information.

'Well,' I said, 'I need to get upstairs. Work to do, Sylvia. I'm sure you've got a lot of work, too.'

So of course she got down to it. 'Why the hell are you chasing after Burkhart's wife?'

'We've talked a few times, so what?'

'About what?'

'She's a nice woman. I like talking to nice women.'

'She's a conniving bitch.'

'Really? Gosh, I didn't get that impression at all.'

'Look, asshole, what's really going on with you two?'

'Ah, the Sylvia Fordham I know and love. "Asshole" is pretty mild for you.'

'I have a right to know.'

My laugh penetrated the darkness like the beacon of a lighthouse. 'You do? And by what right would that be?'

'Because Rusty's my candidate and anything that affects him affects his wife. And it's very strange that you and his wife have been seen talking together at least twice.'

I wondered if she knew about Mrs Burkhart and David Nolan. *Their* meetings.

'Why don't you ask Mrs Burkhart if you're so interested?'

'Because I'm asking *you*.'

'Look, Sylvia. I meant what I said. I have a lot of work to do and I know you do, too. Tonight's the big night for both sides. There's a lot of prep still to be done. There isn't much point sitting here trying to find out something from me when I don't have anything to tell you.'

'Bullshit.'

'I met her a few times completely by accident and we did our best to be civil about the campaign. That's all.'

'You're already lying. The girl at campaign headquarters said that you came there specifically asking to see Mrs Burkhart.'

'I remember asking if that was Mrs Burkhart. She's a good-looking woman. But I did not ask to see her.'

'You're lying.'

I was on my feet. 'Always pleasant to see you, Sylvia.'

'You bastard. You're lying and you know it.'

The waitress materialized and said, 'Will there be anything else?'

I smiled at Sylvia. 'She'd like three more of what she's been having.'

Behind the waitress's back Sylvia flipped me off.

TWENTY-ONE

In my room I went through all my e-mails, most of which I deleted. That penis enhancer I'd ordered had worked so well that I'd had to buy all new trousers. If I bought another bottle of the stuff I'd have to start wearing trench coats even indoors to hide my new love powers. None of this was true but this was basically what some unnamed guy said in the advert that they e-mailed me. Apparently the guy was planking everything female that moved and the women were circling back for more twenty-four/seven. 'Yes, I want to be a STUD!' Just check here and leave your credit card number. But the fun was over. I hit delete.

The phone calls came back to back. First I heard from Nan Talbot, Lucy's friend at the small-town newspaper. I'd asked her to see if she could find anything about the rift between Ward and Nolan back in '93.

'I found three stories about their relationship. Two of the stories refer to the falling-out, but without any details. I asked one of the old-timers here and he said he'd been told by somebody who knew both of them that it was over a girl Nolan was dating in college. I guess Ward managed to get her into bed. Nolan didn't know this for a long time but one night the girl got drunk and told him everything. So he and Ward had this falling-out and didn't speak for a long time.'

No surprise. Ward's psychology was as mysterious as ever to me. Was having sex with his best friend's woman his way of showing that he was the superior of the two? Or was it just that he couldn't keep his hands off women and gave no thought to their relationship with other men? I remember a movie star of Golden Age Hollywood vintage saying that when you bedded a married woman you felt a real sense of accomplishment. Like climbing a mountain, I guess.

'The most interesting thing is that Nolan's first client was a guy from the other party. A guy who was running in the primary. If he'd won he would have faced Ward. So it would have been Nolan versus Ward. That would have been interesting.'

'No kidding. But then they got back together again later on, right?'

'Yes. But there's no indication why. I guess just because they'd been friends for so long.'

'Thanks, Nan. I really appreciate it.'

I was just starting across the room to the fridge for a cold V8 when the phone rang again. It was Matt Boyle, the whiz kid/oppo man from Silberman-Penski that I kept on retainer.

'Now a lot of this was known the first time Burkhart ran for governor. But I've fleshed out some of it here. Teresa Burkhart, aka Susan Wallace aka Nicole Steele or Teresa Sievers, her real name. Sievers was born 1980, Billings, Montana. Father managed a lumberyard, mother a clerk at a dress shop. Teresa Sievers attended Montana State for two years then dropped out to go to New York. Did some minor modeling but no real success. Became the mistress of a prominent attorney. Moved to the West Coast after a few years and tried acting. Was in a few local commercials. Again only minor success. Hooked up with a reality show producer and was his mistress for two years. At this point she was Susan Wallace. It was under this name that she met Rusty Burkhart. The pattern here's pretty clear. A kept woman who really enjoys the good life, as they say. She has one problem. The rumors are that all of her affairs with rich men ended because she always had younger men on the side and eventually got caught so she got dumped. This might be the case with your Burkhart, but I have no way of knowing. But she's married this time so she should have a big payday in store if anything goes wrong. Oh, by the way, she went back to her real name, Teresa Sievers, when she married him. Hard to say if she wanted to start off being honest with him or if she didn't want to give him any legal grounds to avoid a big divorce settlement. Marrying under a false name would put her in some jeopardy.'

'You were right. She gets her big payday.'

'Less if he can nail her. From the little I know of him he probably had somebody do a background check on her before he married her so he's no doubt been keeping an eye on her. A guy his age and a trophy wife – especially after he dumps his wife of thirty-six years – he's got to worry about karma even if he doesn't know what it means.'

'Yeah, they focus grouped the wife dumping. Even the conservative women who liked him otherwise had some doubts about him because of that.'

'They were thinking about their own husbands dumping them for a young one.'

'Exactly. Well, keep looking. You might turn up a little more.'

I shaved again, showered, put on the successful middle-aged guy gray pinstripe with the white tab-collared shirt, the red power tie, the black socks, and the dependable Midwestern black oxfords. Macho doesn't do much for me but I've never been able to figure out why some men like tassels on their shoes. Tassels should be reserved for strippers.

Then came the first of several surprises for the night.

She was downright prim in a royal-blue sheath dress, black cashmere coat, black heels, and black leather gloves. She presented me with a smile, a bit strained, true, but pleasant nonetheless, and a proffered hand, which confused me. Was I to kiss it? Thankfully, she just allowed me to shake it with my own hand.

'May I come in?'

I thought of how well the Japanese were doing with robots. This one obviously came from their new line of Mrs Burkharts. The nasty ones had endured scrap metal death.

'Something I can help you with?'

An injured tone. 'I thought maybe we could be friends. You sound mad.'

'Not mad. Just curious.'

'Well, the least you could do is invite me in. I don't exactly like standing in the hallway.'

I stepped aside. She usually moved with a self-conscious sweep; tonight she was more modest. Smaller steps and no grand gestures. She said nothing until I closed the door.

'Well, Mrs Burkhart, what would my brand-new friend like to drink? But remember, we've both got to be at the debate in a little while.'

She laughed. 'You're always a smart ass. And I'll take Scotch if you have it.'

As I poured our drinks, she took off her coat and gloves and laid them neatly across the armchair. Then she seated herself at the table.

After I brought drinks to the table and sat down, I said, 'You wouldn't be wearing a wire, would you?'

'You mean one of those things for recording people?'

'Uh-huh.'

'You really think I'd do something like that?'

'It's possible.'

'You must have a very low opinion of me.'

'Not any lower than my opinion of Mussolini.'

Confusion in the arrogant brown eyes. 'I take it that's one of your snide jokes.'

'I'm still trying to figure out why you're here.'

She'd been holding her drink. Now she set it down. 'I'm afraid you're going to go to the police. I can't find David and everything's getting scary.'

'Is this Susan Wallace talking or Nicole Steele?'

I'd expected a dramatic reaction. I was almost disappointed. A rueful smile. 'Oh, great. This is really getting ridiculous. I just told you that everything's getting scary and now you bring up the past. How did you find out?'

'An investigator I use.'

'There should be a law against those people.'

'Why are you here, Mrs Burkhart?'

'Will you please quit calling me 'Mrs Burkhart'?'

'You were following Waters and taking pictures of him. Why?'

'Because I thought he might have something I wanted. David thought so, too.'

'So you and David were on good terms? A man from the rival campaign?'

'Would you fix me another drink?'

She lit a cigarette while I was tending to the liquor bottles. There was no point in arguing the hotel's no smoking policy. Royalty makes its own rules.

'Thank you for making this one a little stronger,' she said, holding the glass up for observation, like a jeweler with a gem. 'I need it.'

'You were going to tell me about you and David.'

She took a deep breath, closed her eyes, and moved her lovely lips silently. I wondered if she was saying a prayer, the way basket-ball players do before a free throw. 'I know all about my husband Rusty going to a whorehouse down the river. He charged everything to a Visa account he thought I didn't know about. I started matching the dates of his nights away with the dates on his Visa bill. It was the same 'Allied Supplies' account over and over. After five years he was bored with me sexually. I wanted to make sure that I got all I could when we split up. I was at a party at the governor's mansion one night. One of the few people there from your side was David Nolan. He looked miserable. I liked him. I'd been completely faithful to Rusty. I guess I wanted to show myself that I could still do it. But there was something about David I really liked. He was very masculine but he seemed open, too. I could see he was in pain. Rusty wasn't there that night – probably at the whorehouse – so I suggested to David that we go out for drinks after the party. He was pretty cute. He thought I was going to pick his brain to get some secrets about Jeff Ward.

'We both got so drunk we told each other all kinds of things. I told him about how my husband went to this whorehouse all the time. And then he told me that Ward went to the same one. We had a big laugh about that. But otherwise he was pretty bitter – he told me how he suspected Ward was sleeping with his wife, though neither of them knew that he knew. We realized we had a lot in common – we wanted to get back at the two people running for the same congressional seat. Another thing I liked about David was that he took me seriously. Rusty had checked me out before we got married. Because of my past he treated me like a bimbo. But I've been taking online classes for years from the University of Illinois. I'm close to a BA in hours. I've been studying English and history. For some reason Rusty thinks this is very funny. He thinks he's such a brain, but he never got past freshman year himself.

'Anyway, that night David and I went to a motel and had a very nice time. And when we woke up in the morning we decided to go ahead with our plan. We'd hire a private detective to get proof that Rusty and Ward were regulars at this whorehouse. David even wanted interviews with some of the girls. The detective called us and told us he had what we needed. Then he tripled the price we'd agreed to. We said we'd pay him. But when David drove to Chicago to get the DVD the detective had just died. David went to his office and managed to find what we'd paid for. He brought it back here and made a copy for me. He had his in his desk. He went out for a late dinner one night and when he came back it was gone. He was convinced that Waters took it. Waters was the only one in the office that night for one thing, and David was sure Waters had overheard David and I talking about it on the phone. He said that Waters snuck around a lot, trying to get things on people. I started taking photos of Waters. I wanted them to give to this other investigator we were going to hire to check him out.

'And then poor David found out his wife had been sleeping with Ward. He just went crazy – even though he'd suspected all along, when he confirmed it he just came apart. He called me the night he found out. I'd never heard him like that. I was afraid for him.'

'You haven't heard from him?'

'No. And I'm afraid something's happened to him.' Then: 'I need to find the other DVD so I have the only copies. I want to divorce my husband. I want a big settlement. I can't have that other DVD floating around.'

'What about the money you already got from him – and from Jeff Ward?'

'What the hell are you talking about?'

I took a large swallow of my drink and said, 'You and David were blackmailing them. Between them, they paid you both a lot of money.'

'Well, maybe we earned it.'

'So you're admitting you blackmailed them.'

'We didn't look at it as blackmail. We were just getting even.'

'I wouldn't try that one in front of a jury.'

We sat without speaking for a full minute. Her head was down.

'We have to find David,' she said. Then: 'Just please don't go to the police. Neither my husband nor Ward is in any position to say anything about the blackmail because if they do, everything will come out. You're the only one who can hurt us. So will you give us a break?'

'The way you gave your husband and Ward a break, you mean?'

'I guess I deserved that.'

I was on my feet before I said, 'I need to get ready for the debate. And so do you.'

'So what the hell does that mean?' The brand-new friendship was starting to fray. This was the old Mrs Burkhart, and she was *muy* pissed.

'It means I'll think about it.'

'You're a real son of a bitch, you know that?' She was gathering her coat and gloves. 'I come up here and I'm completely honest with you and look what I get.'

Her charm and honesty hadn't worked. She had to be wondering if tearing her clothes off wouldn't have done the trick instead of her helpless female routine.

I took her by the elbow and walked her to the door. She tried ripping her arm from my grasp several times. I liked her better this way.

I'm sure she was going to lacerate me with more insults, but when I opened the door there was a group of hotel guests in the hall. She decided not to give them a show.

TWENTY-TWO

You might have mistaken the evening for a movie premiere done on the cheap. True, there was only one spotlight prowling the star-spread night sky and none of the people queuing up in front of the double doors could be said to be glamorous. But the patriotic music over the loudspeakers gave even old ops like me a distinct thrill. And photographers and TV crews were grabbing shots of everybody they could find.

When you thought of how many people around the world were murdered for even asking for an event like this – cowardly and rote as some of the events were – you had to feel that despite the bankers and the bought-and-paid-for Congress and the haters and the madmen . . . as yet we still had a country that we could rightly be proud of.

So the venerable building with the ivy binding much of it was tonight a symbol of many honorable things, even if the two men who would take the stage were slightly less honorable than some of the slaveholders and opportunists who signed our Declaration of Independence. For all that I disliked him, Jeff Ward would still stand up against the worst representatives of both parties.

Now was the time for a smoke, standing in the clean October air and watching the movie-premiere spotlight play across the sky while the earliest arrivals – who just might be movie stars if you didn't look too closely – filed into the building. These would be the people who'd gotten advance questions from ops on both sides. Ops wanted their advocates as close to the stage as possible. Political signs were prohibited here as was any kind of campaigning. The people went in quietly and without incident. I imagined they were surprised to find metal detectors were in place. The sponsors didn't want a tragedy or even a near-tragedy to mar the night.

Kathy Tomlin came up next to me and said, 'They're taking bets at this little bar I go to sometimes. It's kind of blue-collar. They're betting that Burkhart pounds Jeff into the ground.'

'That makes sense. Burkhart would pay them ninety-eight cents an hour if he could get away with it. No wonder they like him.'

'I say that to them. If I was a guy they'd punch me. All I usually get is, 'You're a crazy broad,' while they're staring at my breasts. Which is better than at my father's country club. I worked as a waitress there one summer and it was like working in a greaser bar. They thought they had a right to keep touching me.'

'Sounds like my kind of place.'

'Would you care to get a drink as soon as this is over? And that's not a proposition.'

'I'd like that very much, Kathy.' Then: 'Ready to go inside?'

'I wish I still believed in God. I'd say prayers for Jeff.'

Even with an hour to go, the auditorium was filling up quickly. There were two sets of seats, each eight across, with a wide aisle between. Near each wall was a stand-up microphone where the questioners would stand. My guess was that the organizers were afraid that if there was only one shared microphone there might be trouble. Our people were on the right side of the place. We took seats in the fourth row from the front.

'I hate that he won't let anybody see him,' Kathy said as we sat down.

Usually two or three people from the campaign are in the dressing room of the candidate, prepping him and encouraging him until just before he has to go on stage. Ward was different. According to Kathy, he always got to the site early and then barricaded himself in whatever room had been prepared for him. The only person allowed in was the makeup person. And he or she was told to make it quick. Neither Kathy nor Lucy liked this idea, but I understood it. Getting bombarded with last-minute ideas would only increase my nervousness and I assumed that was the case with Ward. Silence allowed you to focus. I knew a candidate who brought ten-pound hand weights to his dressing room. He exercised for an hour. It relaxed him.

There were so many TV people on stage they resembled an ant army. There was some trouble with lighting the four reporters who'd sit on the panel. Crew members sat in the empty chairs while the director and a man on a tall ladder with wheels tried several different angles with the lights. A giant screen had been mounted above stage central so that the audience could be seen in close-up.

Lucy slipped in next to Kathy. She smiled at us then held up her crossed fingers. She leaned forward so she could see both of us and said, 'There are some demonstrators outside. Burkhart's people. One of them shoved one of our people and our guy shoved him back. The police arrested both of them. I just hope the night goes all right.'

Comedians use the term flop sweat for when they bomb with an audience. I get something similar when my clients have to go on stage for a big event. And mine usually starts about half an hour before that insidious little red light appears on the camera.

I'd been in situations like this where one group taunted the other group across the aisle. Tonight there was a begrudging civility. Down front people from the opposing parties were even making a show of shaking hands. Best behavior for the TV audience. The stations were grabbing shots even before the debate began. The dust-up outside had already given them the moment of confrontation their news managers would demand. Politics had more and more begun to resemble professional wrestling encouraged by the TV people. Who wanted to watch anything as boring as a serious story where there was no battle or strife?

Lucy and Kathy talked quietly while I opened my laptop and checked up on our other campaigns. One of our two oppo guys had turned up a twenty-year-old DUI arrest on our opponent. Our guy wanted to know if he should try and get in touch with the arresting officer in case our opponent had given him any kind of trouble. Worth looking into but a twenty-year-old arrest could cut both ways. I could see our opponent 'fessing up on the tube with his family and the required number of American flags behind him as he said, 'And that was when I learned my lesson about drinking and driving. Something I've told my two teenage daughters over and over. Drinking and driving – there's no excuse for it. And I haven't done it once since that night twenty years ago.' We would have just handed him a good-guy moment and managed to look a little sleazy in the process. We might use it anyway but it wasn't really strong unless he'd decked the arresting officer. Or at least tried to.

At a quarter before the hour the moderator, a former Chicago anchorman who now fronted infomercials, appeared on stage. He had to ask three times for the audience's attention. Infomercials do not inspire respect. When they finally started listening he ran down all the rules for the evening. The big two were Don't Applaud and Don't Make Any Derogatory Noises when you disagree with something a candidate says. Then he did a mini-testimonial dinner speech about the billionaire funding tonight's debate, which I would have liked much better if he hadn't twice said, 'And even if he agrees with one candidate more than the other – he thinks it's time for a new start in government – he wants both sides to get an equally fair hearing.' Gosh, I wonder which candidate he favors?

Then he got into the subject of asking questions. That segment would run half an hour, the debate itself fifty minutes, with five minutes each for closing arguments. He said that if any question sounded inappropriate the microphone would be killed instantly, and that the questioner would be escorted from the building. He sounded adamant about this and I believed him.

The cameras picked up the moderator who had now moved to center stage to shake the hand of each reporter who walked to the desk. Two men, two women. Two from Chicago, one from a suburb, and one from a farm town.

The tension and the thrill of the moment was on most faces as I looked around the rows behind me and across from me. Many of the conversations died; eyes were on the stage now.

'This is an honor for me,' said the moderator, who had walked from the front of the desk to the center of the stage. 'I spent twenty-three years covering Illinois politics in cities and towns of all sizes. I even managed to survive in Chicago for nine years without being shot or put in jail.'

Not a bad line; got a good laugh.

'Tonight we have as our guests two men who represent very different views of our federal government. Since we get most of our information from sound bites, I'm hoping that tonight our panel and the candidates themselves can talk about their beliefs in more detail. As many of you probably know, after the candidates give their five-minute opening remarks, some of you will get to ask them questions directly. We can't accommodate all of you but we will get as many of you to the microphones as we can.

'Right now I'd like to thank Mr Richard Anderson for making this possible tonight. I want to thank all of you in the auditorium and all of you tuning in at home. This is the kind of event that helps keep our democracy strong. And now without further ado—'

Burkhart came from the right, Ward from the left. Both men got standing ovations from their supporters. And there weren't even any applause signs to generate the enthusiasm. For once Burkhart wore a suit, banker's blue with a somber blue necktie. He appeared no less fierce. Ward, by contrast, could have stepped out of an adventure novel involving a fortune in diamonds and nookie. His smile redeemed him. It was just boyish enough to make you forget that he was probably the kind of guy who wouldn't lend you a hand after he'd accidentally run over you.

Finally the moderator had to step forward again and raise his arms for silence. Three times, he said, 'The clock is running, folks. We've got to move things along.'

Burkhart gave the first opening statement. There was nothing new in it – he basically wanted to privatize everything up to and including police forces (today's police forces had nasty unions) – but whoever was writing for him had cut way back on the invective. He still sounded crazy to me but he was crazy uncle crazy, not psycho crazy. He even managed to work in a joke about a bureaucrat. His side threatened to give him another standing O.

When it was Ward's turn I thought of all the videos of his previous speeches I'd skimmed through. He didn't need any help from me. He was a natural performer with good instincts. No cornball, no preaching. A clean, incisive style coupled with the good looks and a light sense of humor. One thing I'd noticed in going through the speeches was that they'd gotten a lot better lately. And tonight's opening remarks were the best of all. He talked about our grandfathers and their sacrifice in the big war. And how our grandfathers had gone through college on the GI Bill. And how many good things had come from the government funding so many programs to help get America going again after that tragic war. I imagined even some of Burkhart's supporters agreed with Ward's words.

I leaned over to Kathy and whispered, 'Jim Waters outdid himself with this one. He wrote a hell of a speech.'

Before she could respond the moderator said, 'All right. We're going to start the questions now. Remember, while we expect them to be pointed we also expect them to be civil. If our director feels that any of them are offensive to the audience here in the auditorium or at home, he'll cut the microphone. Let's begin with a question from the challenger's side. Step up, please.'

The people had been chosen, the questions written for them. First up was a young man in a Marine uniform. Sylvia was doing her job. Next up would likely be an ageing nun. With a limp.

'This is a question for Congressman Ward. Congressman, you say you support our fighting men and women involved in the war but you constantly talk about how the war is a waste of blood and money. Since you've never been in the military yourself, aren't you undermining all of us who fight over there?'

Loaded question, fair question. But Ward was prepared. He'd been called a 'traitor' by most of the neocons many times so he knew how to handle this one. He noted that most of the neocons who wanted endless war had never served in the military either. 'Which is worse? Me asking for the lives of our children not to be wasted? Or for the neocons constantly trying to put our children in harm's way? It's rarely *their* children of course. They prefer sending other people's children.'

A small ripple of applause played across our side. But the moderator was quick and stern. 'No applause, please.'

First up for us was a middle-aged man in a wheelchair. The microphone had to be adjusted for him. I'd asked Kathy for a man with an especially sad case for our lead. She'd found him.

'Mr Burkhart, you've said that one of the first things you'll get rid of when you go to Washington is all the "feel good" programs. You want to privatize Social Security "sometime in the future", to quote you, and you want to have savings programs instead of Medicare. I'm a thirty-nine-year-old former biology teacher and football coach. Two years ago I was hit with cerebral palsy. I wouldn't be here today if it wasn't for the "feel good" program that has helped me and my family just get by. Would you cut off people like me?'

Burkhart handled this better than I would have predicted. 'There would be a fund of a billion dollars for special cases. And the fund would be constantly kept at that level. There would be help for those who really needed it but we'd get away from big government giveaways and red tape.'

Spoken with measured and friendly tone; a seemingly reasonable man with a sensible approach. Here and at home his supporters would be nodding their heads. *We knew our man would show this pretty-boy lefty hack how the government should be run.*

Presumably, someone in the press would, tonight or tomorrow, point out how laughably insignificant a billion dollars was when you were trying to bring help and justice to the medical problems of a nation of three hundred million strong.

Burkhart's next questioner didn't need to wear a hard hat for us to know he was a hard hat. The one problem I had – and I hoped others had – was that he pushed the stereotype too hard. 'When me 'n' the boys at the construction company talk about all the filth that's bein' taught in our schools, we wonder where it's goin' to end. You're for sex education startin' in high school. And that means all this gay stuff. One of the boys said that should be for the parents to tell the kids, not the teachers. What about dat?'

Dat? Really? I knew a good number of construction workers from working with different unions over the years. I had never met any who said 'dat' for 'that.' In fact, I had never met any who sounded like Rocky Balboa here. I was surprised he wasn't scratching (or scratchin') his balls and pickin' his nose by now. This guy had to be a local actor of some kind; real local. And a plant.

Our second questioner was a prim, pretty middle-aged woman in a blue skirt and a modest white blouse. She had the kind of earnest bright sweetness that made right-wing talking heads chortle and point fingers. Some dumb middle-class white broad who didn't know shit about keeping America safe.

To Mr Burkhart, she said, 'I'm a librarian and I have to say I find your idea of privatizing libraries deeply offensive, Mr Burkhart. Libraries hold a very special place in our country's history. There's probably not a man or woman in this auditorium tonight who hasn't spent many, many hours in their local libraries. And your idea of hiring people who've never been trained as librarians just to save money – I'm not worried about my job. I'll get by no matter what happens. But I'm worried about all the fine librarians I've met who'll be put out of their jobs – and all the communities that will suffer because of your idea. Would you please speak to that? Thank you.'

I was certain that Sylvia had a list of crazy ideas he'd have to defend. His supporters wanted blood and thunder and she had likely schooled him on wrapping everything in big government wasted spending. But when he started responding to the librarian his voice was softer than usual and he spent a full minute backtracking on his pledge to privatize libraries. 'I always used that as an example. I didn't ever actually say that I was thinking of privatizing libraries per se, only that I'm pretty sure some of these librarians who've been there a long time are probably kind of coasting and not earning their money.'

Burkhart had just stepped into three inches of horse shit. While his supporters heard their man get harsh the way a real man gets, there would be a minimum of ten newspaper columnists and numerous TV editorialists who would nail his ass for attacking librarians. He seemed to understand this. He looked unhappy when our next questioner stepped up to the mike.

The man's slightly stooped back and long, mussed gray hair suggested he was at least in his sixties. Kathy's whisper to Lucy was loud enough that I could hear it. 'I don't remember him from the rehearsal.'

'Neither do I.'

The man was tentative. He might have been afraid of the microphone because he kept his head angled away from it when he spoke. He cleared his throat before speaking. His words cracked when he spoke. 'This is a question for both of you gentlemen.' He doddered when he walked; he doddered when he spoke. There was something wrong here. Somehow the voice was practiced, not real. I stared more carefully at the man. The dark overcoat was so big for him it was cape-like. The hair was, I realized, a wig. Who the hell was he?

'Proceed, sir. We don't want to run out of time for questions.' The moderator allowed himself a hint of irritation. I wondered if he'd also concluded that this guy was a ringer of some kind.

After two more clearings of throat and one more dramatic leaning away from microphone, the would-be old man said, 'There was a case in New York not long ago where a famous politician was forced to resign because he was found to be a regular visitor to a house of prostitution. If both of you were found to be guilty of the same crime, would you resign?'

I lifted up at least two inches in my seat. My impulse was to race over to him and see who the hell he really was. He spoke in a code that both candidates and I understood. Maybe two or three others in the building knew what he hinted at as well. Then the name came to me and a millisecond later, as Kathy clutched my arm, his identity was confirmed. 'It's David; David Nolan.'

This time I did leave my seat. People on both sides gawked at me. Leaving a political debate for any reason was apparently as unthinkable as leaving a Mass the Pope was saying.

The two security men in their blue uniforms leaned against the front doors. One of them worked a BlackBerry; the other stopped scratching his balls when I came through the interior door.

'Help you with something?' the ball-scratcher said when it was obvious I wasn't going to the john or walking out through the front door.

'I'm just waiting for somebody.'

He shrugged.

Burkhart was responding to Nolan's question. 'This is exactly the kind of behavior I'm going to change when I get to Washington. This country was founded on the principle of family comes first. The Founding Fathers were examples of how we were supposed to live our lives. Look at Washington and cutting down that cherry tree.'

I wondered if he'd ever been abducted by aliens. Or maybe Santa Claus. Could he possibly believe that hokey false tale about Washington and chopping down that tree?

Ward was much better. 'I don't want to comment on anybody else's morality – we've got too many so-called "moralists" judging people today – but I do think that as a matter of professional ethics, it's dangerous for a politician to put himself in a position where somebody can take advantage of him. I've spent my two terms in Washington working for the greater good – for the decent men and women who are suffering today because of the excesses of the super-rich and their foot soldiers – and that's a full-time job, believe me.'

God alone knew what any of that bullshit meant but it sure sounded good. Burkhart's face was squinched in displeasure. He knew a good pitcher had just thrown some of his best stuff of the night. But both men probably needed an EKG. They knew that somebody was on to them. If Kathy and likely Lucy had recognized Nolan, Ward probably had, too.

A questioner from Burkhart's side had now positioned herself in front of the microphone. My assumption was that Nolan would leave the auditorium after he'd shaken up the two candidates. I watched him leave the microphone but instead of coming up the aisle he turned to a curtained area on the wall and disappeared inside.

'Is there an exit on the right side down by the stage?' I asked the BlackBerry man.

'Yeah. And we've got a man posted outside there.'

By the time I reached the front doors I was running. Cold air, smells of exhaust fumes, nearby burning leaves, soggy earth from recent rain.

The stretch between the front of the building and the side door was a lot longer than it appeared. Or at least it seemed to be as I ran it. A portly blue-uniformed man stood there watching me come closer, closer. He went for his walkie-talkie.

When I reached him he took two giant steps backward. I'd always wanted to be a pariah.

'Did an old man just come through that door?'

'What's it to ya if he did?'

'He's my father. He's suffering from Alzheimer's. He wanders off sometimes. He just got up and left the auditorium before I could stop him. This could be really serious.'

'That stuff's bad. I'm sorry.'

'Did he come through here?'

'Yeah. I think he was headed toward that parking lot over there.'

'Thanks.' I started running again. The lot he'd mentioned was across the street. Most people attending the debate parked here. In the pale purple glow of the security lights the flanks of cars formed an impenetrable barrier. No sign of Nolan. Maybe he'd already left the area. Maybe he'd never entered the parking lot. Maybe he'd seen me talking to the security man and was crouched between two cars, watching me.

I had to enter the lot. Nowhere else to look now. As I crossed the street I saw the headlights of a van come alive with alien stark-ness. Easy to imagine Nolan behind the wheel. Backing out.

The van was five rows deep and on the edge of a lane. I stumbled and slammed into the side of a new Buick trying to get to it. I shouted at it. I heard the whine of the reverse just as I reached the fourth lane. He completed his backing and pointed the green van in the direction of the closest exit. I didn't have any choice. I ran for the lane he was in and just as he started pulling away I reached his vehicle and pounded on his window. Or rather, her window. A very comely blonde in an IHOP uniform. She gave me the finger and then sped away.

Have you seen this man? I'd be the police sketch of the day tomorrow. I hoped they'd be kind enough to make me look both handsome and erudite.

Making an ass of yourself saps your confidence. I didn't resume running. Or even searching. I just stood there boiling in my shame.

I didn't trust Mrs Burkhart; too crazy. But Nolan could bring it all together for me. Maybe he could even tell me who'd killed Jim Waters. Or maybe he'd *admit* to killing Waters. I had to find Nolan, shame or not.

I walked the lines of cars. The light created shadows and the shadows deceived the eyes. Too easy to imagine sounds and the things that could lurk in those shadows. The one thing that most of the cars and SUVs and vans had in common was their age. Few of them were more than two or three years old.

It was then I saw him. He still wore the dopey wig and the cape-like topcoat. He had misjudged how well he was hiding. He was two lanes away hunched down and hurrying toward the rear of the lot. It might have worked if his head hadn't popped up for a second. He, too, was imagining sights and sounds and he'd paid the price for his misjudgments. After a time all the parked cars became a maze.

I went after him. 'Nolan! Stop!'

He wasn't foolish enough to slow down and look back at me. He was a heat-seeking missile now. I was running again but he reached the street before I did. Traffic was heavy and fast. He chanced the kind of dash that should have ended with an ambulance and half a dozen flaring squad cars. But he made it. When he reached a grassy empty lot he didn't slow down. I was stranded on the edge of the curb watching him disappear into the shadows of an alley that might as well have been in Cleveland. At that moment it seemed that distant.

I had to make my own chancy dash, the problem being I didn't have the same luck Nolan had. I cleared the lane closest to me but when I was two steps into the far lane a small panel truck material-ized like something from those old *Star Trek* episodes. It was all furious lights and furious horn. If this had been a cartoon the truck would have been standing on its hood, upright.

No way to tell if he was flipping me off. I waved in apology and kept on grinding. Close up the grassy lot was pocked with numerous holes that could do damage to a walker, let alone a runner. It was also a litter box for various animals. Fresh shit tainted the cool, fresh air. The alley probably dated back to the early part of the last century. The garages were all one-car and all the wooden fencing dragged the earth. There were no lights in any of the houses I could see only from the back. This might well be a condemned block. Ghosts from long-forgotten decades crept inside the garages for respite from the wind. If you listened closely you could hear Benny Goodman.

Had Nolan kept running or was he hiding in one of these small crumbling structures? I slowed to a jog, snapping my head right to left as I moved. No cars. No suggestion of people.

Then two garages ahead of me a sharp clap of wood on wood.

When I got in the garage myself, I was able to see what had made the noise. He'd been hiding in the shadows near a door that led to the backyard of the house. Trouble was he slapped the door shut when he made his break and it was that noise that alerted me.

I dove into the darkness, tripping on tire ruts in the dirt floor that had been dug by time and water. Moonlight outlined the sagging door for me. I didn't make the mistake he did. I closed it quietly. Rusted clotheslines, brown dead grass, a storm cellar door. No sign of him.

The first thing I checked was that cellar door. The padlock made it certain that he hadn't used it. Then I was on the street gaping both ways as I had in the alley. Far down the long block I saw the silhouette of a creature racing away.

I raced right after him. After a time the staved-in sidewalk started yielding treasures. Here a gray wig, there a dusty topcoat and finally a greasy, dark-green fedora. I left these gifts to the dogs and cats and squirrels of the neighborhood.

Traffic in this dead area was slight so the sounds of my pounding footsteps were loud enough to bounce off the ramshackle houses as I passed them. Was he aware of me by now?

Three blocks down, this street fed into a major avenue. I was getting close when I watched him turn to the right and disappear into a blaze of light that leapt from buildings into the night sky. Some kind of neighborhood business strip.

I turned the same corner in time to see him cross the street and rush down past two taverns and a video store. This was a block of small businesses destined for urban renewal. Half the front windows were dark. The people on the street were shuffling silhouettes emptying from the taverns, heads down, shoulders slumped. Not even alcohol had cheered them.

A cracked and taped window promising 'Pizza' turned out to be Nolan's destination. As he reached for the door his head turned and our eyes met. Even from this distance I could see his panic. After shedding his old-man clothes, his gray V-neck sweater, white shirt and black trousers marked him as a middle-aged professional who was out of place on a street like this.

The traffic was dense here, too. Two signs indicated that the interstate could be picked up just one block from here. It wasn't quite nine o'clock yet. The cars drove fast as if they wanted badly to be out of this neighborhood.

By the time I managed to reach the other side of the street he'd been inside 'Pizza' for three or four minutes. If he was still inside.

The smell of pizza was the only appealing thing about the long, narrow, and swollen-walled place. Tiny tables with red-and-white-checkered tablecloths made not of cloth but oilcloth lined both walls. The pizza ovens were in back, fronted by a counter where two men in white T-shirts stood talking in an agitated way next to the cash register. When they saw me their eyes narrowed with suspicion. He must have warned them I'd be coming.

None of the customers showed more than momentary interest in me as I hurried to the counter. Even before I quite reached it the bald one said, 'We don't have anything to do with it. You want him – he went out the back door.'

'You're not a cop, are you?' the other one said.

I didn't answer. I was too busy rushing to the Exit sign. Outside again. A long alley. And there, in the distance, he ran. As I started after him I wondered how long we could keep going. We were obviously both in decent shape but we weren't exactly athletes. Was one of us just going to flame out, fall face first on to whatever texture of ground we were running on, and lie unmoving until the cold night air began to plug our sinuses and rasp our throats?

He turned left at the head of the alley. I was grinding through space, blind animal pursuing blind animal. In my imagination at least he had begun to slow some. Or I was finding a remarkable second wind?

This time he resorted to what he must have thought was a very tricky trick. As I reached the street he went left again. He had assumed I wouldn't get to the street in time to see where he was going. He had also assumed that I would assume he'd turned right into a street filled with condemned houses ripe with winos, rats, and hiding places.

What he'd done was lead us right back to the dreary street of the taverns and 'Pizza.' Except this time he was running in the opposite direction. When I hit the street I saw that I hadn't imagined his lagging strength. He was no more than half a block away. If this had been even ten minutes ago he would have been at least a block or more from me. He had one advantage, though. He knew where he was going.

And soon enough I knew where he was going, too: the interstate. When he reached the end of the street he took a sharp right and started climbing a small hill that led to the entrance. As he scrambled up toward the green-and-white sign he glanced back at me. He seemed to give a small jerk as he realized how close I was. Then he was up and over and I couldn't see him for the moment.

The hill was more imposing than it appeared. Twice I had to dig my fingers into the dirt to keep my footing. And once I stumbled and gashed my knee on an unseen rock. Or maybe it was a piece of glass.

The interstate. Rush and roar. Music flung from cars. Tiny cars living at the mercy of the behemoth eighteen-wheelers. Video games with American and Japanese and Korean vehicles. Gleaming colors against the rolling Midwestern darkness.

I got to the top in time to see it. His idea was to find an opening in the rush of traffic and make his way across the two lanes here, stop and wait for a break in the lanes on the other side and then leave my sorry ass far, far behind.

He came breathtakingly close to losing his life trying to cross the southbound lanes. He miscalculated the speed of two oncoming cars. One of them had to swerve to avoid him. If car horns could curse, that horn spat out every dirty word ever concocted.

The choice was to let him go or try my own suicide run. Vehicles blasted past me fast enough to make me lean away from their force. Several good citizens, seeing me standing on the edge of the concrete lanes, flipped me off. One teenager was creative enough to flip me off with both middle fingers. A Rhodes scholar in the making. I of course had never done anything that asinine in my own perfect teen years.

The dumb bastard was going to try it. Nolan teetered on the edge of the grass between south and north lanes ready to jump as soon as he saw what he took to be a reasonable chance of making it.

I'd come too far to let him disappear again. Now I started looking for my own reasonable chance. If I got very lucky I could catch him on the grass before he had the opportunity to race across the lanes closest to the woods on the other side.

I had two false starts, both attributable to this vision I had of becoming instant roadkill. When I finally got to it I put my head down and plunged on to the huge roadway. Horns were already blasting me when I was only halfway across.

Because I had my head down and was concentrating exclusively on surviving, I didn't see the accident. More horns, these from the far lanes. And a scream that must have made the stars tremble. And then a sound of collision. Car and body.

By the time I stood where Nolan had just been I saw the nearest of the two lanes clogged with stopped cars. A man was running from his car, his arms flailing in the air. I could see what he was about to find. Later the driver told the press that Nolan had been knocked maybe seven or eight feet in the air before smashing to the roadway. Right now the man knelt over the bloody rags that had been Nolan's clothes and shouted at him as if trying to resurrect the dead.

I walked over to him, joining a dozen or so other drivers and passengers who'd come to see what had happened. Through his torn trousers a white bone poked; his right ear had been half ripped away. His chest heaved and blood bubbled in the corners of his mouth. I thought he was trying to say something.

I didn't bother to introduce myself; I just knelt down next to him, dislodging the man who'd struck him.

'Nolan.'

The eyelids fluttered but never lifted.

'Nolan.'

'You know him?'

'Yeah.'

'Did you see it, the accident, I mean?'

'Yeah. You couldn't help it. I'll testify to that.' Well, I didn't actually see it but I still knew this man wasn't at fault.

'My wife's already called 911.'

'Good. Now leave me alone here, will you?'

'Sure.'

He got up, middle-aged knees cracking, and was immediately surrounded by the others.

'Nolan.'

Again the eyelids fluttered; again they refused to open.

Before he left he spoke only one word I could understand: 'Ward.'

TWENTY-THREE

I saw a woman on TV once who claimed that she could see the souls of the newly dead leaving their bodies and seeking the light only they could see. She said she saw this most often when she visited hospitals, something she didn't do unless a loved one was sick, because watching the souls flee the dead frightened her. This came to mind as I stepped off the elevator on the third floor of St Francis Hospital, where surgery was being performed on David Nolan.

Mrs Nolan was in the waiting room. She glared at me as I started to enter. I did us both a favor and joined Kathy and Lucy in a small grotto-like cove down the hall. This was an older section of the hospital. I wondered how many hundreds of people had waited here for the appearance of a doctor to bring them his or her verdict. I could almost tap into all the relieved smiles as well as the shock and disbelief and horror of those who wouldn't be smiling for a long time.

There is no silence like hospital silence. It is easy to imagine the classic Grim Reaper in his hooded attire slipping into rooms at random and smiting sleeping patients with his scythe and dispatching their souls to the next realm. The three of us sat on a small tufted gray couch between framed paintings of a maternal Virgin and a weary Jesus. I sat between the women. Kathy touched my hand and said, 'It should have been Jeff, not David.'

Her bitter words preceded by seconds a fleeting sob of Lucy's. She hadn't acknowledged me as yet. She stared off at something only she could see. And she kept fingering a small gold cross.

One of the police officers at the accident scene had let me ride with him to the hospital. I was there half an hour before Bryn Nolan slammed into the small office where I was talking to the surgeon who'd operate on Nolan. Without hesitating, she pointed to me and snapped, 'I want him out of here. This is my husband we're talking about. And this man is no friend of mine or my husband's. I wanted to call the police about David being missing but he wouldn't let me.'

Since I'd pretty much passed myself off as a coworker of Nolan's, the graying doctor's face tightened in confusion and then suspicion. He wasn't up for a war. 'Maybe you'd better leave, Mr Conrad. I appreciate your help.'

'I want to know everything he told you.'

Even crazed Bryn was an appealing sight in her soft white sweater and jeans, her hair in one of those perfect chignons that upper-class women wear as badges of honor. But crazed she was. Did she really think I would've said, 'You know, Doc, Nolan's wife was humping the shit out of his best friend.' Damned unlikely.

There was nothing to say. I left. I used my cell phone to call Ward's father and got an answering machine. I left a message and told him to call me no matter what time it was.

After fifteen minutes in the cove with Lucy and Kathy, I took the elevator to the ground floor. The cafeteria was closed but there were, mercifully, two pots of free coffee. Neither Kathy nor Lucy had wanted any. As I rode back upstairs on the elevator, a cup of coffee in my hand, I started worrying about how we needed to play all this to the press.

Reporters would soon find out that Nolan had been the disguised man asking the question about prostitutes. They would also soon find out that Nolan hadn't been at work. Campaigns break people; they'd be wondering where he'd been. I've come close myself at times. The days and nights become one and they become endless. You are in a war and the enemy never stops firing. You are constantly backing and filling. And then securing enough ammunition to attack on your own so that the other side spends its time backing and filling.

When I got to the cove I found Lucy quietly crying and Kathy noshing on one fingernail. I was left with no real idea of what was going on. A private detective had videotaped material destructive to both Ward and Burkhart. Mrs Burkhart and David Nolan had conspired and paid to have it done. The private detective died unexpectedly. Nolan raced to Chicago and found the material he wanted and brought it back here. The idea was to blackmail both candidates. Vengeance on the part of both Mrs Burkhart and David Nolan. And then Jim Waters had stolen the DVD and was going to blackmail them himself. Then Waters was murdered. But who murdered him, and why?

'I wonder what's taking so long,' Lucy said.

'You heard what the doctor said, Lucy.' Kathy laid a sisterly hand on Lucy's arm. 'This could take hours.'

Lucy's blue eyes shimmered with tears. 'There's a chapel on the ground floor. I've been to Mass there sometimes. I think I'll go downstairs and light a candle for him.'

After she lifted her purse and got to her feet, her gaze came to me and rested there for a time. As if she was trying to deduce something. I couldn't tell what her eyes were saying. Maybe she was angry; maybe she thought, as I had, that if I hadn't been chasing Nolan he wouldn't be on the operating table right now.

But then her mouth broke into a quick, shy smile and she turned and headed for the elevator.

Kathy and I sat there without saying anything for a time. The unseen shoes of nurses squeaked down hallways somewhere on this floor. Faint conversations could be heard up at the nurse's desk. Elevator doors opened without dispatching anybody, then closed.

Kathy said, 'You notice he's not here.'

'Ward?'

'Yes. He's somewhere with a bimbo and after he's done he'll sit up all night trying to figure out how to play this to the press.'

'I was doing that myself.'

'That's your job. Besides, you haven't hurt David the way he has. David's sort of old-fashioned in a nice way. He and Ward would always have it out when Ward started sleeping with staffers. David really hated that.'

'I hadn't heard about that.'

'Oh, yes. Jeff is compelled to try and get every female staffer into bed. He got me as far as his motel room when we were on the road one night, but I sobered up before we could do the deed. He wouldn't speak to me for a week or so afterward. The worst part was when one or two of the younger ones fell in love with him. They'd end up crying on David's shoulder. He didn't know how to handle it. Who would?'

I was beginning to understand the breadth of the problem of handling Jeff Ward. So many ways he could be brought down. 'At least his opening remarks tonight were really strong. Waters could really write.'

'He could before Jeff tried to fire him. Lucy saved him. She started writing all his stuff for him. Turned out she was better at it than Jimmy was. Jeff didn't know about it.'

'Jimmy seemed bitter when I talked to him.'

'He was. Every time we'd have a conference and Ward would compliment him on how good something was, Jimmy'd look at me. He knew that I knew, that Lucy had confided in me. Plus he resented her for sleeping with Ward.'

'Lucy did?'

'Yes, she used to call me up nights. She was always crying. They'd been sleeping together for a few months before I knew anything about it. She actually asked me if I thought he'd leave his wife for her. I've got a little sister who's naive like that. I wanted to cry myself when she talked that way. I imagine Jimmy did, too. He and Lucy had gone out for so long they'd been talking about moving in together. Then she was in Washington for a couple of weeks and she came back and she was all starry-eyed.'

Starry-eyed, I thought. What a terrible way to feel when you're in the clutches of somebody like Jeff Ward. But then I started thinking about Lucy and Jim Waters. If they were intimate then she'd probably known about the DVDs and if she hated Ward for dumping her . . .

In my army days I saw a lot of bases and a lot of chapels. Every so often I'd park my lapsed Catholic ass in a small chapel – never a church – and just sit in a pew for fifteen or twenty minutes. I liked the theatricality of Catholicism. The red and green and gold votive lights and the deep dancing shadows they cast on the walls. I liked it especially when the scent of incense was still on the air.

Now I thought about Erin and how much I loved her and how frightened I was for her. A schoolboy Our Father found its way to my lips.

At this hour Lucy was alone in the chapel. It was short and narrow. All the lights had been shut off but the doors remained open. There was a single line of pews. She sat in the front row.

I took a seat in the pew behind her. It was so dark in here the altar was lost in all but rough outline.

We sat in the sad silence for several minutes. The only sound was that of her occasional sighs. She cleared her throat before she spoke. She didn't turn around. 'Any more news on David?'

'Sorry. You know as much as I do.'

'Poor David. He got drunk one night and told me what Jeff and his wife had done.'

'Is that when you knew Jeff wasn't going to marry you?'

Her head tilted downward. 'I guess Kathy told you. It just makes me feel stupid is all, what I did.'

'I'm sorry you were hurt, Lucy.'

'I'm thirty-four years old. Jimmy laughed at me when I told him we were breaking up because of Jeff. He said he knew he was nerdy but at least he wasn't naive the way I was. I shouldn't ever have left him.'

'But you went back to him. And he told you about the DVD he'd stolen from David.' A conjecture, but a reasonable one.

'Jim was going to blackmail them. He wanted me to help him and then we'd run away and get married. He was in love with me; we'd been sleeping together for a long time. I wasn't sure if I loved him but I liked the idea of getting back at Jeff. But he wouldn't do it. He got scared. All his big talk and his big plans, but when it came right down to it he wouldn't do it. He just kept saying we'd go to prison. He got real paranoid. He even managed to get a gun somewhere and kept it in his car.' I thought of the .38 bullets I'd found in one of his bureau drawers; now I knew where he'd kept the gun. But the police hadn't found it in his car.

'You wrote his speeches for him.'

'He had some kind of block. He wrote a couple of bad ones and Jeff started riding him. And that intimidated him. He couldn't write anymore. I didn't want to see him get fired. Is that how you figured out how I knew about the DVD?'

'When I found out I started thinking maybe there was a connection. If you were close enough to know about his block, you'd probably be close enough to know about the DVD.'

After a time, she said, 'When I was little and my parents got into their fights I'd always run down to the church and sit in the chapel. They had terrible fights. I got so I'd be afraid to go home. But sitting in the chapel with just the candles always helped me. Like nothing could touch me as long as I was there.' Then: 'I leaked a lot of stuff to the Burkhart campaign. I really wanted to hurt Jeff. Now I wish I hadn't done that.'

So I finally had my spy.

'I hate to say anything at a time like this, Dev – I mean poor David's being operated on and here I'm worrying about myself – but do you think I'm in any legal trouble?'

'Not if nobody ever finds out. Just about every campaign has a leaker once in a while. You should be fine.'

'But I still feel guilty anyway. I wish I'd been nicer to Jim, too, and I wish I'd never known anything about that DVD. I think I really would've gone through with it.'

'Maybe not. Maybe at the last minute you would've changed your mind.'

'But I was really tempted.'

'We're all tempted to do all kinds of things. But we don't do them. That's what matters.'

I put my hand on her shoulder. 'C'mon, I'll walk you back to see Kathy. She's probably worried about you.'

'Sometimes this is all like a dream,' she said, then stood up and carefully made her way out of the pew. She made a quick sign of the cross, then turned to me and said, 'Even if we win, I'm going to quit. I can't take any more of him, Dev. I really can't.'

TWENTY-FOUR

I n my hotel room I checked my messages and drank a beer. The wind smashed invisible fists against the windows. For a time I thought about Erin, about how much I'd been in love with her and how, as I'd learned talking to her again, at least some of those feelings remained. Her dying seemed impossible. Not in this time continuum, not in this universe. She was too fiercely alive to ever not exist in earthly form. Then I thought of our daughter and what she was going through now. The same fears I had.

The surgeon had told us that David's surgery had gone well. The evaluation would continue tomorrow with a neurologist brought in. I'd said my goodnights and come back here.

I needed to change the subject. Jenny's cell phone rang several times before she answered. The clamor made me hold the phone away from my ear. Banging band, shouts, laughter, cries.

No point in trying to recreate the conversation. It was interrupted several times, once by somebody apparently trying to grope her. I had to repeat four times exactly what I wanted her to do. She finally seemed to grasp what I was saying and began to sound suspicious. Or maybe not. Maybe I was imagining it. Hard to say. She was in a club not far from my hotel. But she agreed. Half an hour. The bar downstairs.

The place was crowded. Another convention, this one of certified public accountants, began in the morning and the early arrivals had decided to throw back a few in the quiet, respectable way one would hope CPAs would conduct themselves. No one had barfed on the bar yet or goosed a waitress or thrown a punch. That might come later, but looking around it seemed unlikely. These guys didn't even raise their voices when they drank. These people were downright un-American. Or maybe it was simply the fact that a good number of the CPAs were women, almost always a civilizing factor except on the dimmest of American Express cowboys.

She was twenty minutes late. The male CPAs paused in their quiet conversations to note the fact that a fetching young woman had entered their purview. She'd given up on Goth and now wore an expensive black coat and black heels. She began to take her coat off before she reached my booth, revealing a smart black dress. I wondered if Armani had a line of mourning clothes.

Only the hair and face were the same, a hint of fashionable street girl and Eastern college coed. The only difference now was the lack of luster in the dark eyes and the grave gray circles beneath them. Her sigh sounded weary when she collapsed into the booth across from me. 'God, thanks for calling. I just couldn't seem to leave that place. I hadn't been there in a long time and all these creeps I used to hang with wouldn't leave me alone.'

A waitress appeared. I asked for another Scotch and water. I expected underage Jenny to order Perrier or the like but she said, 'A glass of merlot, please.'

The woman, at least as weary as Jenny, glanced at me. I shrugged. 'I'll have to see some ID, miss.'

'Oh, sure.' And from within a shiny black purse slightly larger than a pack of cigarettes, Jenny's hand secured a red wallet. She flipped it open and offered it up. The waitress's eyes went from the ID to Jenny and back again. She returned the wallet with a 'Thank you, miss.' She took one more look at me, knowing she'd been bullshitted.

'How much did that cost you?'

'It's a pretty good one. Two hundred and fifty. I haven't been turned down yet.' Jenny should have been sounding boastful, insolent, but not tonight. And it was just then that I noticed she'd started biting her lower lip; I also noticed the quick look of apprehension now filling the eyes.

She knew why I'd asked her to come over here.

'I miss Jim. I even called his number a couple of times today just to hear it ring. Isn't that crazy? I'm glad they haven't disconnected it yet.'

'We all do stupid things when we're suffering. Right after my dad died I used to put on one of his sweaters and pair of shoes and walk around in them all day.'

'That's pretty sad.'

'I suppose, but at the time it was comforting.'

The waitress was back with our drinks. As she set Jenny's drink down, she said, 'Honey, whatever you paid for that ID, you spent too much. But this is the only drink you're going to get from me tonight, okay?'

After she was gone, Jenny said, 'They never hassle me about it at clubs.'

'They may have paid off the cops and don't have to worry about it.'

'You're always so cynical.'

'Practical. That's how a lot of clubs operate, otherwise they'd be out of business.'

'I thought I looked older, anyway.'

'Not tonight you don't. You look exhausted – and scared.'

The last word jolted her. She had been about to raise her glass of merlot but then stopped. 'I don't know what I'd be scared about.'

'Sure you do.'

She gripped her drink hard enough to whiten her knuckles. 'If you keep looking at me that way I probably will be scared. Are you drunk or something? The only reason I came here was because I thought you'd make me feel better.'

'I'm trying to help you, Jenny. I called our old friend Pierce earlier and he told me something about the night before Waters died.' I'd had to promise to mail him a hundred-dollar bill in the morning.

'You believe anything that creep has to say? You know what kind of pervert he is.'

'Yeah, I do. I'm not saying he's a wonderful guy but I believe what he told me.'

'Can't we talk about something else? I just want to relax. This hasn't been an easy time for me.'

'Pierce said that the night before Waters was murdered, you and Jim had an argument so loud the other tenants called Pierce and complained. But you told me you hadn't seen Waters for two days before he died.'

'Did you ever think maybe I forgot? I'm not exactly thinking straight these days, you know?'

The Jenny I'd first met in Waters' apartment wouldn't have whined like this. She would've insulted me and smirked. But this was a whipped nineteen-year-old who seemed to have no serious defenses.

'Listen to me, Jenny. I know you killed him. You may not have wanted to, but there was the gun in his car and you knew about it. You'll feel better if you tell me about it.'

'God, I can't believe you're saying this. Of course I didn't kill him. I loved him.'

'But he loved Lucy and you knew it. And you're a woman who gets her way.'

'Oh, I see, I'm some spoiled rich bitch who killed some comic book nerd because he was in love with somebody else. I know what this sounds like but I'm going to say it anyway. I loved him but I always felt I was doing him a favor. I'm not beautiful but I'm pretty good-looking, or at least a lot better-looking than the girls he would've been able to get. And he knew it. I scared him. He was afraid I'd dump him, that's the only reason he started seeing that Lucy. I could've had him back any time I wanted him.' The energy her bragging took impressed me. She was rallying now, the little girl lost behind her mask of arrogance. But it was over quickly enough. 'I thought you liked me.'

'I do. That's why I'm trying to help you.'

'By getting me to admit that I killed Jimmy? That's a real big help.'

'By telling the truth. Maybe one of you got that .38 from his glove compartment and then something happened that neither of you meant to happen. Maybe he was threatening you with it to leave him alone – or maybe you were threatening him with it to take you back.'

It might have been a gag in a magic act, the way she produced her cell phone. It wasn't there and then it was there. Where the hell had it come from?

'I want to call my father.'

'You're not going to talk to me anymore?'

'Not when you talk crazy like this.'

'You know I'm not talking crazy. I don't believe you killed him intentionally. I'm giving you the benefit of the doubt.'

'My father will know what to do. He always knows what to do.' The father she mocked? The father she at least pretended to despise? 'You'll be sorry.' She was nine years old again now. She thumbed a single number.

I heard the phone ringing. Once, twice, three times, four times. 'I'm sorry it's so late. You need to help me, Daddy. This terrible man is saying terrible things about me.'

She decided to intimidate me with her master's voice. She put it on speaker phone and held it up so I could hear him.

In the background I heard a sleepy woman asking what was wrong. 'You hear that, Jenny? Now you've woken your mother. What kind of trouble are you in this time? Jesus Christ, what time is it?'

'Is she in trouble?' the woman said.

'Just let me handle this,' the father snapped. 'Are you drunk or on drugs as usual, Jenny?'

'I just had a few drinks.'

'A few drinks. That's what you've been telling us since you were fourteen.'

She realized now that letting me hear her old man talk hadn't been such a good idea. He had one of those boardroom voices: manly, angry, definitive, as if he was God's own representative here on earth.

As she started to cry, he said, 'Oh, Jesus, don't start that.'

'What's she doing?' The mother's voice was concerned.

'She's crying. She always cries. It's part of her act when she gets into trouble and I have to take care of it for her.'

Jenny's hand had lowered, the phone with it. It seemed to grow heavier the angrier her old man sounded.

I said, 'Your daughter's in trouble and she needs you to help her right now.'

'Who the hell is that?' he bellered.

I took the phone from Jenny's hand. She offered no resistance. She slumped in the booth, placing both her hands over her face.

'My name is Dev Conrad. I'm in town here for a few days working on the Ward campaign.'

'The Ward campaign? What's my daughter got to do with that bastard?'

'She'll tell you all about it when you come to the Royale Hotel and pick her up.'

'I seem to remember buying her a very expensive Porsche about eight months ago.'

'She needs a goddamned ride, all right? I seem to remember she's your daughter.'

There was pain in the pause. Maybe he wasn't as bad as he'd sounded at first. Leery now, he said: 'What kind of trouble is she in?'

'Nothing you want to talk about on the phone.'

'Oh, God.'

'What's wrong, Tommy?' the mother said, picking up on his tone.

'Now we're going to sit here and in twenty minutes go to the lobby where we'll hope to see you in the drive-up waiting for her.'

'Make it a half hour.'

'Make what a half hour, Tommy?'

'Will you shut your fucking mouth?'

I'd been wrong. I guess you couldn't take the Tommy out of old Tommy no matter how hard you tried.

I handed the phone back to Jenny.

'I really appreciate this, Daddy.'

Her mother was sobbing in the background. She didn't even know what was going on yet.

After she closed her phone, Jenny said, 'It really was an accident. I just hope somebody believes me.' She shuddered. This time the dark gaze was timid, fragile. 'You see what I mean about my father?'

'Yeah,' I said, 'I see what you mean about your father.'

'I shouldn't have said that about Jimmy being a comic book nerd. That's one of the reasons I loved him so much. He accepted me for what I am and I accepted him for what he was. We were really friends, too.' Then: 'You think that waitress would give me a bourbon and water? That's what I drink when I get serious.'

The waitress was laughing about something with three people at a nearby table.

'Probably not. But how about if I order it and you drink it?'

'My father really isn't as bad as he sounds sometimes.'

'I'll order you that drink now, Jenny.'

'In other words, you don't like him much.'

'If I say I don't like how he treats you and your mother, can we change the subject?'

'Maybe I should get a double shot.' She tried to smile but couldn't quite pull it off. 'It really was an accident, Dev. It really was.'

TWENTY-FIVE

As I pulled in behind headquarters I looked at the approximate spot where Jim Waters had been killed. Jenny had explained it to me as we waited for her father. Waters had told her how much he loved Lucy. In a rage she pulled the gun from the glove compartment, not meaning to kill him, just to frighten him. But he'd lunged for it and the gun had gone off. I wondered how many times this particular tale had been told to skeptical cops within the confines of interrogation rooms. Maybe it was true. I liked to think so because I cared about Jenny and because no matter how hard I tried I couldn't imagine her killing anyone.

I got out of my rental and walked over to the spot, the whipping wind proving a bitter foe determined to fight me. I'd seen one of those paranormal TV shows one beery night in which a female psychic claimed that she could contact a murdered person simply by standing on the place where he or she had been killed. A handy skill. If I possessed it all I'd have to do is call out Waters' name and he could clue me in about what had really happened.

The back door of headquarters opened and a voice, tattered by the wind, said, 'I knew you'd show up here tonight.'

'I'm trying out a paranormal trick I saw on TV. I planted that thought in your mind.'

Kathy laughed. 'You don't really believe that stuff, do you?'

I started walking to her. 'Not really. But you never know.'

When I got inside, she said, 'I've got coffee on upstairs. He's in his office screaming at people on the phone.'

'Anybody I know?'

'First he called Lucy. Now he's yelling at his father. He blames him for sending you here. He seems to believe that everything was going fine until you showed up.'

She smelled of woman warmth, tender perfume, and faintly of bourbon. I wanted to kidnap her.

'I may as well get it over with.'

I followed her exquisite shape up the stairs. She steered me into her office where she had one of those four-cup coffee brewers on a table near a stack of paperback novels. 'Sometimes I just close the door and read. I need the escape. I put headphones on so I can't hear anything. If something really goes wrong they pound on my door and I hear them.' She handed me a cup of coffee. It smelled rich and good. 'I get these beans at a boutique in Washington. I buy a three-month supply at a time.'

The first sip reminded me of why I enjoy coffee. In all the slush you get most of the time you start to forget how good it can be.

I could hear him bellering down the hall. Too far away to pick up the exact words but poor baby did not sound happy, that much was for sure.

'You going to stick around for a while?'

A girly grin. 'Where would I go? I have no other life. I'm in politics, remember?'

'I'll go talk to him and then we can go have some drinks.'

'I'd like that. But the mood he's in, I may have to take you to the ER.'

'I'll be fine, Mom.' Then: 'All right if I take this?'

'Sure. Just bring the cup back. I only have four of those.'

By the time I reached Ward's office there was silence. Easy to imagine Tom just hanging up on him at this hour. Ward was probably trying to figure out who to rag on next.

I knocked with knuckles and walked in before he could say anything.

When he saw me, he didn't curse or shake his fist at me. He just smirked. 'Well, well, the Angel of Death.'

'Yeah, it's pretty much all my fault, all right. I made you screw all those women in Washington and then hang out in a whorehouse about seventy miles from your hometown. And let's not forget how I pushed you into screwing your best friend's wife. That was genius on my part.'

'Yeah, and what did the son of a bitch do to me? Put me on the spot tonight in front of the whole district. If he had a problem with me, he should've been man enough to face me instead of dressing up like a bum and trying to humiliate me.'

'I see. You're the victim, not David?'

'Don't give me any of that Oprah bullshit. You know damn well what I'm talking about. I'm trying to get re-elected. I'm fighting the good fight, in case you've forgotten. And I was doing all right until my old man forced me to work with you. Or haven't you noticed that? You show up and everything goes to shit. You couldn't even find out who was selling our secrets to Burkhart.'

I wasn't about to hand Lucy over. 'I admit it. I did a bad job with that part of it.'

'You did a bad job period. Here I am working night and day while you're messing up everything my old man promised me you'd fix. I'm the only pro here; I'm the only one who knows how to run a campaign.'

Yes, sleeping with your campaign manager's wife is the mark of a true pro, all right. One thing about megalomaniacs, they rarely have a sense of humor. Or have any perspective about their actions. When I got here, he was running behind and he was being black-mailed. He'd been on a roll, no doubt about it. 'Yeah, you were in great shape till I showed up.'

At this point he was wearing a black crew neck sweater and jeans. Cool dude. He shoved his hands into his pockets and smirked. 'I see Kathy favored you with one of her coffee cups. She hates me so I don't get any. Some staff, huh? David, Kathy, and Lucy all hate me.'

'Gosh, and you're so easy to love. Who woulda thunk it?'

But I'd pushed poor baby too far. He extracted his hands from his pockets. He used one of them to slam down on the desk he was standing next to. 'What the hell're you doing here? I'm sick of your face, I'm sick of your name, I'm sick of my old man telling me how good you are, and I'm sick of you undermining me.'

I finished the coffee and set the cup on a small table stacked with recent newspapers. I was as sick of him as he was of me. 'I'm going to make this fast, asshole. So listen carefully. I think you're going to win this one. It'll be a squeaker but you're going to win. Then you'll go back to Washington and one month after the new House session starts, you're going to announce that you won't be running again.'

'Oh, yeah, right, I'll be real sure to do that.'

'I'm told there's a young guy in this district who has a lot of promise. A primary challenge would be messy and hurt his chances in the election. But when you make your announcement, he'll have the time to start raising money and meet the people.'

No smirk; just scorn. 'You're out of your mind.'

'If you don't do this, I leak the DVD and you'll be done anyway.'

He started around the desk but I was ready for him. When he came at me he was off balance so all I had to do was give him a shove. He landed in one of the comfortable chairs facing the desk, but he was anything but comfortable himself. He started cursing me with such fury that he didn't take the time to make his curses coherent. Finally he snapped, 'You're blackmailing me, you son of a bitch.'

'Right. And I'm getting the same message to Burkhart. If he runs again, the DVD gets fed to every TV station in the district. He's CEO of a very big corporation. He couldn't stand the heat.'

He began to rise from the chair. He looked surprised that I didn't shove him back down. 'You'll never get away with this.'

'Sure I will.'

'Not after I tell my old man what you're up to.'

'When I tell him everything he'll be on my side. He did something similar to this to one of his own clients years ago. He knows the turf.'

I walked back to the table and picked up my coffee cup. 'It's over, Ward. You've got one term left. Do it with a little class. You and your wife can still live in Washington and hang out in Georgetown or wherever's hot at the moment. You can keep on screwing all the women you want and the press won't care anymore. All you'll have to worry about is pissed-off husbands.'

'Listen to me, Conrad. Think this through. Burkhart can't release the DVD because I'll do the same to him. We're in a stalemate. I'm protected. As long as you keep your mouth shut.'

'No, we're not protected, Ward. You're the one who's not thinking it through. Nobody knows how many copies of these DVDs are floating around out there. David and Mrs Burkhart hired a private detective to get the video. They didn't know much about him. By now they could be all over the place. That's how these things always work. You think you're safe and suddenly some TV station has them on the six o'clock news. The party can't risk that. You're done.' I looked straight at him. 'And like I said, if you don't announce that you won't be running again, I feed the DVD to the press while our new candidate still has time to mount a good campaign.'

He was flustered now, shaking his head as if trying to escape a nightmare, hands fluttering around his head. 'This is insane. The party needs this seat.'

'The other side'll have a fresh candidate after Burkhart loses and we need one, too. You're damaged goods, Ward. Your little affair with Bryn'll come out and then you'll be toast. So get ahead of it all and announce that you won't run again. It'll be better for everybody.'

I walked to the door. Opened it. I looked back and said, 'Nice knowing you.'

I was six or seven steps down the hall when I heard him run to the door where he shouted, 'You're crazy if you think I'll go along with this!' He slammed the door with enough force to make the floor tremble.

Kathy had her coat on when I replaced the coffee cup on the silver tray in her office. 'It sounds like you guys are better friends than ever.'

'Almost blood brothers. But he wouldn't let me cut his wrists for him.'

She giggled and kissed me on the cheek. 'God, I'll be glad when I don't have to work for him anymore.' Then: 'Let's go get drunk.'

I was leaning over and packing my bag when Kathy came out of the bathroom, all showered and fresh. In her white hotel bathrobe, she made it tempting to take a later plane.

She walked over and slid her arms around me as I finished my packing. She smelled clean and cool and wonderful. 'I hope I didn't ruin the night by crying there just before we went to sleep.'

'It's sad, Kathy. It deserves some tears. Waters is dead and a lot of people got hurt.'

I turned around and took her in my arms. The feel of her flesh made me tremble. We got into one of those kissing matches that more often than not end up with both people dropping to the floor and writhing around like crazed animals. It had been a while for me before last night and now I wanted more. My lust was like a lovely ache. But then I had no choice but to pull away. I managed to say, 'Airport.'

She favored me with her great grin while she pretended to fan herself. 'Wow. I should sue you for alienation of affection. You really had me going there.'

'Maybe you can visit me in Chicago for a day or two after the election's over. Then we can get a little crazy again.'

'I'd like that, Dev. I felt very comfortable last night and it's been a long time since I felt that way with anybody.'

'Me, too, Kathy. But now I've really got to go.'

This kiss, this hug, were ones that my third-grade nun would have approved of. 'There'll be a cab downstairs to take me to the airport in five minutes. I already checked out while you were showering.'

She took my arm and squeezed it. 'I hope everything goes all right. I hope they get everything with Erin and I hope you and she have that long talk you've been needing all these years. And if you want to talk while you're there, you have my cell number.'

At the door I said, 'You'll hear from me. Probably more than you want to.'

One hour and twenty-five minutes later I was sitting in my United seat. Right then all I could think about was Erin – how much I'd loved her and how much I feared for her now. Then the plane was lifting and we were heading back to the past.